ALL-KNOWING WITCH

All Knowing Witch
Mountain Witch
Book IV
by Luiza Dobrzynska

Paperback ISBN: 979-8-9922051-4-5
ePub ISBN: 979-8-2301476-5-7
***
Written by Luiza Dobrzynska
Published by Royal Hawaiian Press
Cover art by Tyrone Roshantha
Translated by Rafal Stachowsky
Publishing Assistance: Dorota Reszke
***
Version Number 1.00

ALL-KNOWING WITCH

BOOK IV
MOUNTAIN WITCH

by Luiza Dobrzyńska

TABLE OF CONTENTS

In Aunt Emilia's old house there lives a bad girl
And waiting is lurking in the corners
And in the pub on the corner, they say that at night
A strange stranger comes into the house

"In Aunt Emilia's Old House" –
a song by "Andrzej & Eliza"
lyrics by Bogdan Olewicz

A storm raged over the city. Heavy, near-black clouds churned above the roofs of the tallest buildings. With each flash of lightning, the outline of distant mountains was snatched from oblivion for the briefest instant; when the light died, rolling thunder followed, booming like the barrage of a thousand cannons. Rain slashed down in long, steady sheets, turning the streets into rushing torrents.

High atop St. Mary's Tower, a solitary figure could just be made out. Had anyone noticed them, they would surely have wondered who could settle on the needle-sharp peak of a roof in such devilish weather—and how they managed to remain there with such effortless poise. Perhaps they might even have called the authorities, troubled for the safety of this lonely admirer of storms. Yet no one saw them, nor could anyone have seen them, unless the crouching watcher upon the tower willed it so. Or unless the observer was someone endowed with an extraordinary, near-preternatural sensitivity. Such people have been rare throughout the long history of humankind, though a few have indeed existed. Usually artists. Goethe[1], Bulgakov[2], or that funny poet from Poland, Gałczyński, with whom he spoke in Paris. The Pole even wrote later:

That Devil of Notre Dame

---

[1] Author of the play "Faust".

[2] Author of the novel "The Master and Margarita".

He looked at me and asked:

"Are you Dr. Lam?"

"No, Scythian....[3]"

This was considered a poetic parable. Yes, people can be blind when they want to or when something doesn't suit them.

Neither the driving rain nor the storm itself troubled the watcher. This was his element—something he loved to witness, something that never lost its charm. Besides, not a single drop dared touch his black suit or the beret tilted over his left ear, as though he existed within this world and yet somehow beyond it.

What was he doing here, in Kraków? What whim held him in a city he disliked, in a country that had always struck him as far too sanctimonious for his taste? He—known from land to land as Woland, Ahriman, Lucifer, or simply the Devil—could never feel truly at ease in such a place. So what, then, kept him here?

He could no longer recall the last time he had been so captivated by a woman.

A woman... though in this case one ought to say a barely-grown girl. Not long ago he would have dismissed her as wholly unremarkable, yet the dramatic events he had observed from

---

[3] "Notes from the failed Paris retreat" by Konstanty Ildefons Gałczyński.

afar—never intervening—cast her in an unexpected light. For tens of thousands of years he had dealt with mortals willing to bargain away their souls for a taste of power, for youth, talent, revenge, or even love. Amusing, really, that they always came to him for it.

His power was widely known, acknowledged even by those who claimed to believe in nothing at all. Those, predictably, were the easiest to ensnare. After all, the Devil's most elegant trick was convincing people that he did not exist. Such souls he won with ease, handing them their heart's desire while allowing them the comforting illusion that they paid nothing in return. What was a soul, after all? A fiction, invented for profit—so they liked to think.

Yet he had never met anyone who, blessed so generously by fate, would cast everything aside so lightly simply to save another—even one dearly loved. Such sacrifices belonged to novels and films; in life, they were nearly nonexistent. He, older than any human mind could fathom, had witnessed such a thing only a handful of times. Paradoxically, people found it easier to give their lives than to surrender what made those lives unusual or beautiful. But to relinquish a talent—as rare as a pearl in the desert—and in the span of a single moment become... no one at all?

Ah, very few could manage that.

And it need not have happened. He had offered that stubborn brat help—without trickery, without hidden strings, out of the occasional goodwill even a devil could muster. She had not been required to sacrifice anything. She didn't have to—but evidently she wanted to. He ought to have shrugged it off, yet somehow he could not.

Any demonologist would say that the Devil's soft spot is his pride, his vanity. The Lord of Darkness could not easily accept that a frail, insignificant human fledgling—whose life could be extinguished by a single senseless accident—had looked him in the eye and said, "No."

Just like that.

Had it at least been an act of firm faith, he might have understood. But the girl was practically an atheist, agnostic at best. Odd, perhaps, for someone who had seen both gods and demons, but beliefs rarely change in an instant. The life of that young witch had veered off its path too abruptly; too much had happened in too short a time for her to adapt at once.

He curled his lip in ironic amusement. He hardly believed how deeply it bothered him.

And why, exactly? Because for the first time in hundreds—if not thousands—of years, a human had defied him so openly, face-to-face? It was something new, even... refreshing.

Amusing, in its own way. Children like her feared nothing, but when she grew older…

When she grew older…

Did she truly imagine that uttering that little sacramental "No" would banish Woland from her life forever? Or that relinquishing her extraordinary gift would hide her from him, or render her uninteresting?

He laughed. Thunder echoed his mirth, and a bolt of lightning split the sky.

Oh no. *He* decided when—and how—things ended.

We will meet again, Edyta Gwerska.

CHAPTER I

"In my opinion, you should take the year off," Jadwiga said firmly.

That summer, Villa Jodełka had turned into a veritable "women's kingdom," as Manfred Batory—Fred to those close to him—liked to remark with wry amusement. It was understandable that Jadwiga Gwerska, miraculously saved from disaster, had moved in with her siblings and daughter. Less expected was the arrival of Alinka the nymph, along with her cat, and—more surprising still—Oggy, a female werewolf.

Neither had asked anyone's permission. Alinka, like all nymphs, was far too childlike and scatterbrained for such formalities, and Oggy... well, Oggy had simply appeared one day and stayed. No one questioned her, sensing she must have had a grave reason for leaving her pack of vampires; the unspoken assumption was that she would speak of it when she wished. For now, she wished not to. She kept out of everyone's way, helped at the animal infirmary, and studied Polish with great diligence, but she was no more inclined to confide than a stone wall. Something had happened—something serious, one could only hope not tragic.

"Mum! It's like you don't want me to study at all!" Edi groaned. Regaining her mother had filled her with joy, but at times she felt like a poodle whose leash kept getting shortened. Jadwiga Gwerska possessed a strong, domineering character and treated her daughter as if she were still a small child.

"But of course I want you to," Jadwiga assured her. "It's just that you've been through a great deal lately—too much, really. You need time to work through it, and you won't manage that if you bury yourself in coursework. And don't forget—you are not an ordinary girl, even if you've given up your power."

"Why not?"

"Because no witch will *ever* be an ordinary woman. You think yourself so clever, and yet you fail to grasp the simplest things…"

It wasn't simple at all. Edi had assumed that abandoning her Gift would restore her to the state of a normal teenager, but something in that plan had gone wrong. She couldn't find common ground with her peers, nor muster any real interest in their concerns.

"Fine! I'm coming with you!" Edi brightened suddenly.

"Absolutely not," Janina snapped. "Only witches may enter the Motherwood. You're not even an acolyte anymore."

"So what? Just try to stop me."

The doctor sighed in resignation and glanced at her sister. Once obedient—docile, even—the teenager was becoming more like her mother with every passing day: just as uncontrollable, just as willful. Hard to imagine what she might grow into... but no one, it seemed, had any say in that. Witches always walked their own path, no matter how difficult. Judging by Jadwiga's expression, she agreed.

"Let her go, if she's that stubborn."

"Very well. Then Żywia can decide what becomes of her. I wash my hands of it."

Edi clapped her hands in a burst of triumphant joy. Janina shook her head in disapproval, Jadwiga pressed her lips into a thin line, but neither said another word. Inwardly, both hoped the girl would fail to find her way to the Motherwood on her own, and they planned to slip away from her at the first opportunity. Let her wander and grumble for a while—it might teach her that not everything could be forced.

It was a reasonable plan. It just didn't work.

Edi, as it turned out, had kept her uncanny sense of direction as well as a handful of minor abilities. Not only did she find the path to the Motherwood—she arrived before the Batory sisters. By the time they reached the grove, she was chatting casually with Żywia's new priestess: a not-unattractive woman of indeterminate age, her wavy hair pinned back with a wooden clasp, and burdened with a noticeable excess of weight. The goddess herself did not appear—according to the priestess, conditions had changed. She would explain no more and made it quite clear that the visitors ought to leave promptly.

So, for now, there would be no help from the goddess.

Unable to reach an understanding with her daughter, Jadwiga Gwerska went to the university herself and withdrew Edi's documents. It was perfectly legal—Edi was still two months shy of eighteen and thus subject to her mother's decisions. Jadwiga's action sparked a storm at Jodełka. Edi had never caused such a scene with anyone. She shouted, stomped her feet, and finally locked herself in her room, crying into her pillow like a wounded eight-year-old. She didn't even notice when Kurt, the little willow imp, slipped in through the window. Only when he gently touched her hand did she sit up sharply.

"Oh. It's you."

"Why are you crying, princess? Who dared hurt you?"

The furry creature—smelling of leaves and rotting wood—settled on the blanket and stroked her arm with tender sympathy, his round ruby-red eyes soft with concern.

Sniffling miserably, she told him everything, and Kurt listened attentively, nodding from time to time.

"That's how mothers are," he concluded when she finished. "They always think they know best. Sweetheart, I know you're heartbroken now, but once you calm down, you'll see it's not such a big tragedy. You'll be of age soon, and then Madam Jadwiga won't be able to decide anything for you. Just wait a little."

"But then it'll be too late."

"Nonsense. University won't run away—it'll just be postponed a bit."

"It's already been postponed by a year."

"So what? Work with your aunt for now, study from her textbooks, and you'll have a far better start than other students. Look at it that way."

At last, Edi managed a faint smile and wiped her nose. Kurt might have been a minor figure from Slavic folklore, but as a friend and comforter he was priceless.

"You're such a lovely little devil," she said. "Hard to believe someone like you could be so empathetic."

"You know perfectly well I'm not really a devil."

Kurt smiled too, scampered up to the chandelier, and wrapped his long tail around it. "At least not in the hellish sense. Neither I nor any of my kin serve that realm. When Christianity spread across Europe, people started calling us by those names—devil, imp... just words. We're from the family of *chochliks*, not true demons. Closer to the old Slavic *ubors* and *domoviks*."

He set the chandelier swinging gently and began to sway above her head, making comical faces to cheer her up.

"You know what?" he proposed after a moment. "Come on—I'll take you to a dance. It's already getting dark, so they'll be starting soon. Today is Rusalka Thursday."

"Meaning?"

"The first Thursday after Easter. All the dryads, hamadryads, rusalkas, and nymphs gather at the Witches' Clearing for a grand celebration."

"The Witches' Clearing? Where is that?"

"You don't know? Your aunt never told you? Right at the top of Babica[4]. It's quite close."

---

[4] Babica – one of the peaks of the Beskid Makowski Mountains.

Edi hesitated. It was obvious her aunt and mother would never approve. Janina, in particular, turned oddly old-fashioned whenever it came to dances—she wouldn't allow her charge even the gentlest school disco, let alone the infamous house parties organized by popular girls "when the parents weren't home." Not that Edi cared for them; the reigning queens of the school corridors had no desire to invite her anyway. Still, she had once wanted to go—Ada had asked her.

"The music is too loud and there are strobe lights," Janina had said sternly. "Either could trigger your abilities, and that would be a serious problem. Absolutely not."

Curiously, she felt the same about private parties, though she never explained why. For a more social teenager, such restrictions would have seemed tyrannical. For Edi, however, they provided a convenient excuse when talking to classmates.

Separate from that was Janina's attitude toward Edi's friendly relations with rusalkas and similar beings. She especially distrusted Herta, the one who lived in Crystal Lake. Even the others she tolerated only grudgingly.

"Keep your distance from them," she warned. "Not all are as sweet as our Alinka—and some are very dangerous."

She spoke from experience, of course. But Edi felt irresistibly drawn to the magical creatures that lived alongside the human world, and actively sought their company.

"All right," she decided. "Just wait—I need to change."

One could not attend such a gathering wearing anything containing iron or silver—ideally, no metal at all. Edi quickly removed her earrings, bracelet, and the chain with the titan Krios's crystal, then changed behind her wardrobe door into a linen dress and canvas shoes, the outfit she usually wore when meeting Żywia. For good measure, she braided into her hair the sprig of ever-living rowan the goddess had once given her—a charm said to guard its bearer from all evil. She secured it well among her plaits and stepped out.

"I'm ready."

Kurt dropped from the chandelier and grabbed her hand.

"Then let's fly, princess!"

The floor vanished beneath her feet. Before she registered what was happening, she was soaring through the air at such dizzying speed that it stole her breath. Kurt needed neither broom nor brand to levitate—and to carry another person with him.

The Witches' Clearing, a vast meadow surrounded by ancient spruces, was hidden from ordinary human eyes much like the Motherwood. Not that humans could *never* stumble upon it. Some did, usually by chance or by misusing a powerful artifact. Then everything depended on timing. If no gathering or festivity was underway, the intruder might not even realize what they had discovered. Otherwise, their fate was grim. Rusalkas never coddled trespassers—and dryads even less. Graceful, ethereal, beautiful, they were deadly to those who crossed them.

This did not apply to invited humans, or to those vouched for by invited guests.

Landing at the Clearing, Edi first caught her breath and smoothed her windswept hair, checking whether the rowan twig had stayed in place. Then she looked around.

A great bonfire blazed in the meadow's center, and circles of magical beings danced around it to the music of lutes, flutes, and drums. After a few moments, Edi began recognizing the dancers who whirled past her: *chochliks*, *mamunas*, *biesys*, *nocnices*, *płanetniks*, *boginkas*, *utopces*, *zmoras*, *wodniks*, forest dwarfs, *południces* and *północnices*, sprites, *wiłas*[5], air spirits— everyone celebrated together. Only the Snow Maidens were absent; it was far too warm for them.

Most of the musicians were dryads, lounging on spruce branches as though in hammocks. But soon Edi spotted Latimon the faun with his ever-present panpipes, and Kazo, tapping rhythmically at his bongos. She waved to them—and gasped when someone seized her shoulder. Turning, she saw

---

[5] Creatures from Slavic folk demonology.

Herta grinning broadly, her sharp needle-like teeth glinting in the firelight.

"So you did come! I left an invitation in Jodełka's door, but I wasn't sure you'd find it."

"I didn't. Kurt dragged me here."

"You didn't? Ah, Janina must have taken it away. She doesn't seem thrilled about our acquaintance."

"Thrilled? Lately I can hardly talk to her at all. To Mum even less."

"The eternal problem. For as long as I can remember, human generations have never understood each other. Amazing you've survived thousands of years. Never mind—come, let's dance."

She was pulled forward by her left hand. Another dryad seized her right, and in that instant Edi was swept into one of the circles whirling merrily around the bonfire. She quickly, almost instinctively, fell into the rhythm—a pattern faintly reminiscent of a French farandole—and grasped the strange rules guiding the dance. The rings spun in opposite directions, and whenever the music quickened for a heartbeat, one had to release the hands of their current partners and catch new ones. It all happened so smoothly that Edi could not shake the impression that the dancers were communicating telepathically.

"Oh wow, Mrs. Tokarska!" she exclaimed after one such switch. The hand she had caught turned out to belong to her former high-school teacher—her Polish literature instructor and homeroom tutor. It took her a moment to recognize her, but it was unmistakably her. "What are you doing here, ma'am?"

"You should rather tell me what *you* are doing here."

"I was invited."

"So was I—for years now." The teacher smirked slyly. "Tell me, who do you think I really am?"

"I don't know… Let me think… A *strzyga*!"

"Correct, you little know-it-all. And you never suspected a thing, which means I've been hiding myself rather well."

She flashed a grin full of white fangs. Her students would certainly be astonished to see her now. She looked far younger, wore no glasses, had none of the gaps in her teeth; she might even be considered attractive. And, Edi thought, that had likely caused more than one poor soul a good deal of trouble—after all, consorting with a strzyga rarely ended well for a human. A moment later, the dance shifted again and she lost sight of the teacher.

Someone began a song in a peculiar language, and at once everyone joined in, filling the clearing with a haunting, yearning rhythm that worked on the senses like an intoxicating drug. After several minutes Edi, too, began to sing along; though she neither knew the language nor understood the words, they fell from her lips effortlessly. Within that song she felt again something she had experienced once before—the sensation of merging with the world around her, of being everywhere at once. It was wonderful, overwhelming, dissolving both time and space into a single living tapestry where all things coexisted with all things.

Long past midnight the dancing and singing came to a stop. On narrow benches set beneath the trees appeared roasted meats, cakes, and jugs filled with a pale, glimmering liquid. The revelers threw themselves at the feast. Kurt, who had vanished earlier, suddenly reappeared beside the weary, breathless Edi and caught her by the elbow.

"Don't touch any of that," he warned her in a whisper.

"But I'm thirsty…"

"That's elf wine. That's what they call it, though it has nothing to do with elves. It's not meant for humans. Drink even a little, and you'll forget who you are for an entire year—everything you've lived, gone. I'll bring you some water."

He snatched a clay cup from the bench and slipped into the forest. Moments later he returned and handed it to her. She drank greedily.

"Delicious."

"Spring water. I added fresh mint—grows all over the place."

"Thank you." Edi smiled at the shaggy creature, so much like the little devils pictured in old village tales. "I feel better already. Can I at least eat something?"

"Better not. The rusalki prepared all this, and gods only know what they put in it. They adore spices that are dangerous to humans." Kurt grabbed a piece of cake and bit into it. "Take this one, for example—they added deadly nightshade and henbane seeds. Believe me, you wouldn't want to try it, no matter how good it tastes."

"Well, too bad." She took another sip of the refreshing water. "What happens now?"

"Individual performances. And now, if you'll excuse me, I want to eat something too—and more importantly, drink. Opportunities like this are rare."

He vanished, and Edi sat down beneath one of the spruces, sipping her water. Her legs ached from the frantic dancing, yet she felt wonderful. She had no desire to return home, though she knew she probably should. She preferred not to imagine what would happen if her absence were discovered.

Suddenly movement stirred beyond the clearing. A group of vodnice, led by Herta, dragged someone out of the bushes after a brief scuffle and hauled the captive toward the bonfire amid triumphant shouts.

"Who do we have here?!"

"A human!"

"A spy!"

"What shall we do with him?!"

"Dance him to death!"

"Tickle him!"

"Turn him into a goat!"

"A rat!"

"A stone!"

"Let's just eat him! Like in the good old days…"

"Oh my God, it's Szkrab!" Edi cried in fright, and before anyone could stop her, she rushed forward. "Leave him alone! Mrs. Tokarska, help! It's Wojtek Młyniec! You were testing him on grammar just a few months ago!"

All heads turned toward her in astonishment. The teacher shook her head. She clearly recognized her former student, but had no intention of intervening. Here, at the gathering, she was no teacher—only a strzyga bound by the customs of her supernatural kin. In panic, Edi searched for Kurt, but the willow imp was already half-drunk and unlikely to be of any use.

"Such is the law," said Herta.

The boy, terrified beyond reason, did not even try to struggle. He only rolled his eyes from figure to figure, trembling violently. Herta watched him with her cold, light-green stare.

"Oh yes. I remember now. He was sitting with the others by the lake when I approached them to talk. Your friend, isn't he?"

Edi hesitated.

"That's too strong a word... Just a classmate. A good kid. And a very talented musician."

Herta bared her terrible teeth deliberately. Szkrab recoiled and nearly fainted.

"We understand, but the rules are clear!" croaked Żabka, the grotesque little water-imp lurking in the shadows—shaped like a small child with a monstrously swollen head and bulging eyes.

"Yes, clear!" echoed the others. Only Latimon the faun raised his hand and made a small, dissenting gesture.

"I know, I know," Edi stammered desperately. "I understand... But don't kill him. There must be another way..." Her gaze fell upon the jugs from which the nymphs were pouring the silver liquid. "I've got it!"

She seized one of the vessels and lifted it. A rusalki frowned.

"You think so? And you?" She looked around the crowd. "Our witch friend asks that we spare the life of this pitiful creature, taking only his memory. What say you?"

A murmur of excited voices rose. Some insisted he must be executed; others, more moderate, leaned toward Edi's plea.

"The world is changing," they argued. "We don't have to be what we were centuries ago."

"Tradition commands it!"

"Death to spies!"

"He's just a kid…"

"He's a *human*!"

Herta waited patiently, still gripping Szkrab's collar. Then she whistled sharply through the fingers of her free hand—so piercingly that Edi's ears throbbed. All fell silent at once, and an astonished bat dropped at the rusalka's bare feet. Żabka picked up the squeaking creature and stroked it until it calmed.

"My dear guests," Herta declared, "you are all right, of course. But we must choose only one option. I propose a ballot. What say you?"

Another round of murmurs—then agreement.

"Very well! Prepare!"

All those present—except Edi, who had no idea what was happening—raised their left hands high and straightened their fingers.

"Now!" cried the rusalka.

From the outstretched fingers shot upward tiny glowing spheres—red and blue. Herta examined them closely.

"You're in luck," she told Edi with a smile. "The blue ones are clearly more numerous. Life, not death. Żabka, bring the wine."

The little water-sprite released the recovered bat, which fluttered away into the night, then returned with a cup filled with the silver liquid. She handed it to Edi.

"You give it to him."

"She's right," the rusalka added. "He'll forget about her soon enough."

"Sapkowski had dryads give something like this to kidnapped girls," Edi muttered under her breath, taking the clay cup from Żabka's webbed hands. One of the dryads snorted disdainfully. "Yes, yes, I know—he got it wrong."

She approached Szkrab. She wasn't even sure he recognized her; his eyes were glazed with terror, darting wildly.

"Drink," she commanded, pressing the cup to his lips.

He did not seem to understand, so in the end she had to force the wine down his throat. The result was almost comical: the moment he swallowed the first sip, he grew calm, and all his attention fixed on the cup. Grabbing it, he drank every drop, licked his lips, looked around… then unexpectedly yawned. Herta released his collar and the boy at once curled up on the ground and fell asleep.

"What now?" Edi asked helplessly. She had just realized she could not count on Kurt, happily drinking under the spruces, and she herself certainly could not fly. And even with magical help, she wouldn't be able to take Szkrab with her. "How did he even get here?"

Through the crowd of fantastical creatures pushed Alosza the płanetnik, her good friend. Relief washed over her; he could always be relied on.

"The boy is camping with his friends not far from here, under the yews by the black trail[6]," he reported. "I saw them from above. If the forest rangers catch them, they'll be fined heavily."

"That's the least of their worries right now, Alosza. Especially his." She pointed at Szkrab. "Will you help me? He needs to be taken back, and I must get home before my aunt and

---

[6] Two six-hundred-year-old yew trees, which have the status of a natural monument, grow near the black trail to Babica.

mom notice I've gone out. Kurt won't help—look at him. And he promised to take me home afterward… I still haven't learned to do it myself."

The storm-spirit followed her gaze and smiled indulgently.

"All willow-imps are like that. Show them a full bottle and they forget the world. Not the sort of company for a well-mannered young lady. Don't worry, sweetheart. I'll sort out some transport."

He raised both hands and wiggled his fingers. Above the clearing a low, pale cloud began to form. Edi grimaced slightly. She knew all too well the dubious comfort of traveling on such a thing—like sitting atop a giant clump of wet cotton—but in this situation she couldn't complain.

"Maszka, I'll be back as soon as I drop these kids off!" Alosza called to his wife, who was greedily sampling the feast in the company of a few forest goddesses and chatting merrily. She waved cheerfully and blew Edi a kiss; she was very fond of the girl.

Thanks to Alosza's help, the rebellious teenager's nocturnal escapade remained—for now—a secret from her family, though of course that could not last forever.

CHAPTER II

"Did you know someone's moved into that old House-on-the-Rocks under Wapiennik?"

Nymph Alinka burst into the Jodełka just as she always did—dancing, hopping and practically twirling through the doorway.

Janina frowned. The House-on-the-Rocks, as everyone called it, had been abandoned for decades—or at least that's what people assumed. The truth was that *nobody* knew how old the villa really was. It was certainly pre-war, but *which* war was up for debate. Its architecture was so stylistically neutral it could just as easily have been built in the early twentieth century as in the nineteenth, or even the eighteenth. For as long as the collective memory of the locals reached, no one had lived there, and a few elderly residents swore on all the saints that the gloomy, doom-drenched villa was genuinely haunted. Haunted or not, no one ventured near it, and no one—no matter how determined—would have spent a night inside for all the treasure in the world.

Still, every now and then, rumors circulated that someone did, in fact, live there. No one, of course, ever checked.

Strictly speaking, "the Rocks" were just a patch of wasteland, a stony slope where an unwary walker could easily twist an ankle. Nothing interesting ever happened there, which was why tourists avoided it as well. Nobody remembered who had built the house or why they had chosen that particular spot, and no legends or gossip survived on the matter.

There had to be something unsettling about that villa if neither humans nor animals—nor even the creatures who lived between worlds, like Alinka or ubiquitous Kurt—ever approached it. Only now did Janina realize that she herself had never tried to investigate the mystery. She steered clear of the place like everyone else, and that was that. If the thought of it ever crossed her mind, it did so fleetingly, vanishing almost at once. Even *that* was odd.

"How do you know someone moved in?" she asked.

Alinka, in the middle of an elaborate dance step, froze.

"They took the boards off the windows and put up proper shutters," she explained. "The panes are clean, and I saw light inside. Where's Fred?"

"He'll be back soon. Wait, this is more important. Did you see the tenants?"

The nymph shook her head so vigorously that all her hairpins flew out, and her carelessly pinned hair cascaded loose over her shoulders and back. Like all her sisters, she had astonishingly beautiful hair—long, thick, wavy, a deep honey-gold.

"I didn't see anyone. I didn't even go close. That house gives me the shivers. I don't know how anyone can *want* to live there."

"Humans tend to be remarkably unsensitive... I wonder if they rented the place or bought it?"

"Is that really such a difference?"

Dr. Batory didn't answer. Trying to explain to Alinka the intricacies of property law would have been pointless; she wouldn't have understood a word. Janina, however, knew a thing or two. The deed to the Rocks, although occasionally invoked by various offices, didn't actually exist. The only trace in the city archives was a vague note about a conditional lease. It was phrased so loosely and noncommittally that it wasn't even clear whether the land was being leased from the regional council—or to it. Since at least the end of the First World War, successive authorities treated that patch of land like the proverbial hot potato. Every so often someone came up with a plan to develop it, only for dozens of unforeseen complications to leap out like devils from a box. In the end the matter was always shelved—with barely concealed relief.

And yet someone had dared to break the stalemate.

For some reason this filled Janina with a faint but distinctly unpleasant sense of unease. She would have liked more information, but questioning Alinka any further was pointless. Like all nymphs, she was too childish and scatterbrained to retain anything important. It seemed Janina would have to investigate the matter herself—unless Edyta did it first. Poor girl… Perhaps Jadwiga shouldn't have forced that vacation on her? She had meant well, of course, but her daughter had no desire to "rest." She dreamed of studying veterinary medicine and refused to accept that her mind had been too shaken by recent events. After Jadwiga intervened, Edi sulked for a week, wouldn't talk to anyone, and didn't even ask to assist her aunt. Only when it came out that she had taken part in the gathering on Babica—and Jadwiga gave her an absolutely infernal scolding—did she calm down a little. Perhaps she had needed such a fight to vent her emotions.

Mrs. Gwerska often behaved as though Edi were still a little girl who needed to be led by the hand. Her unbearable bossiness provoked frequent clashes, yet everyone at the Jodełka enjoyed her company, animals included. There was something about her that made life seem simpler, brighter. Her optimism and energy were infectious, and the household—bewitched by her personal charm—usually allowed her to run things however she pleased. Only Edi resisted her mother, especially after Mrs. Gwerska herself withdrew her papers from the university and decreed a one-year break from studies. The girl had become rebellious, snappish, even rude. Every instruction sparked anger, which caused Janina and Fred considerable worry.

"Generational conflict and youthful rebellion—nothing new under the sun," Jadwiga would say dismissively whenever the topic came up, and she truly didn't seem concerned. "She'll thank me someday."

So far, there was no sign of that, though after less than a month Edi had more or less accepted her fate and stopped snarling at everyone. Investigating the House-on-the-Rocks, framed as an important task, might help her recover fully. On the other hand…

There was another matter—something Janina had not discussed with her sister or anyone else. She had only recently noticed it herself and had no idea what to make of it.

According to both her own experience and what she knew from mages, when a witch lost her powers, her body usually began to "catch up" on the years stolen by magic. That was precisely what had happened to Olga Woznańska—and it had killed her. But Edi showed no such changes. Eighteen years old, she still looked fifteen, and nothing suggested that would change. She hadn't lost or gained even a gram, hadn't grown so much as half a centimeter. Something had clearly gone wrong. Janina's priceless book held no reference to a similar case. Truthfully, it was an extraordinary situation: the loss of magical power had affected someone who had not yet truly *become* a witch. A rarity indeed. Perhaps, paradoxically, this had saved Edi from the usual consequences.

But it didn't explain the arrested development.

There was only one possible explanation—one utterly unacceptable in terms of magical principles. Janina felt she ought to consult one of the elder wizards, but couldn't bring herself to do it. Witches had never liked asking men for help. Their magic differed fundamentally from "male" magic, a division that had taken root thousands of years earlier. The result was predictable: wizards often dismissed witches, while witches insisted it was impossible to have a sensible conversation with men. It took truly exceptional circumstances for one side to seek aid from the other. Considering all that, it was hardly surprising Janina decided to wait.

A motor sputtered in the driveway, and moments later Fred burst into the house. In his new black leather suit and helmet he looked like a seasoned biker, though he owned only a lottery-won scooter. He longed for something bigger—a Harley-Davidson, perhaps, or a stylish Honda—but for now he had to make do. Money was perpetually scarce in the Batory household, even though both siblings worked, and their miraculously regained sister contributed her own funds. She never explained where she got them, but every month she topped up Jodełka's budget. Even so, finances were tight. Janina's veterinary practice generated good income, but the costs devoured most of it, leaving little for everyday expenses. And Oxygen, the café-club run by Fred, barely broke even. A motorcycle, therefore, remained a distant dream.

"Hi, Janka!" Fred called, pulling off his helmet. He shook out his tousled hair. "Guess what—the House on the Rocks finally has a tenant!"

"And water is wet. Yes, Alinka told me. She was looking for you—apparently you had a date."

"Damn, I forgot. Senility. Where is she now?"

"As usual—she turned on the radio and is dancing around the living room. And where have you been, you stray?" Janina scolded. She adored her younger brother but his carelessness and lack of seriousness often got on her nerves. "You were supposed to help me at the clinic. The windows are so warped we'll have snow blowing in this winter if we don't fix them."

Fred waved a hand dismissively.

"Tomorrow, Janeczka. Or whenever. And I still don't get why you bother, when a couple of spells would fix everything."

"So you'd have something to ask about, brilliant one! I am *not* giving you a lecture on magical theory. Just know that repairs like these must be done the traditional way, otherwise they won't last... And honestly, you're no help at all since you got that ridiculous contraption." She finished her speech into the empty air—Alinka had darted out of the living room at the first sentence, flung her arms around Fred's neck, and the two disappeared through the doorway.

Janina let out a hopeless sigh and sat on the old bench beneath the hallway wall. If she wanted to be technically accurate, she should have admitted that Fred's natural carelessness had grown significantly *after* he became romantically involved with the lovely nymph—but the timing hardly mattered. The two events had occurred almost simultaneously. Fred had never been particularly responsible, but now he was downright impossible, and she had no choice but to accept it—just as she accepted the behavior of her sister and niece. Lately she felt like the last anchor of sanity in her delightfully deranged family...

Edi, returning from a small gathering at Ada Bielska's, found her aunt deep in thought, sitting with her chin propped on her hands in almost complete darkness.

"Auntie, is something wrong?" she asked anxiously, switching on the light. "Are you feeling ill?"

Janina blinked, disoriented. She realized she must have been sitting like that for hours—it was already evening. She stood up quickly.

"No, sweetheart. My head is simply a mess. Is it really that late? Nobody rang, and I must have dozed off. Damn, I need to do the evening rounds at the clinic—will you help me?"

"Sure, sure. Suddenly I'm good for something?"

"Don't start again. I don't have the strength to argue today. I didn't take your university papers—you're taking it out on the wrong person."

Edi *should* have felt ashamed, but she rarely did lately. A psychologist would probably chalk it up to typical teenage rebellion—albeit a somewhat delayed one—and wonder why she had only now begun to push back against her family. And the exposure to magic, prolonged and intense, would certainly not be the first explanation to occur to him.

The clinic currently housed five dogs, two calves, a cat with kittens, a wolf pup abandoned by its mother, an injured fox, and a peregrine falcon with a broken wing. The last two required caution—they were wild and could easily injure an inexperienced handler. The wolf pup, whose life Janina had fought for over several days, had been adopted by a labrador hit by a car and was now thriving.

"No one's come for her yet?" Edi asked, stroking the fawn-colored dog's head.

"Unfortunately, no. The microchip's inactive. I put ads in the paper—nothing. I think she was simply dumped."

"Poor girl…" Edi inspected the stitched wound along the dog's side, changed the dressing, and felt the mammary line. "Auntie, she has perfectly normal lactation. Is it possible she left her own puppies somewhere?"

Janina shook her head.

"Certainly not. I examined her thoroughly when she arrived. If she'd recently given birth, I would know. Many females start producing milk when they hear the characteristic cry of a young one of their species. Even humans can do it, though rarely."

Edi lifted the wolf pup and studied him. He squirmed in her hands, squeaking, eager to return to the warm belly of the labrador. He looked like an ordinary, helplessly young puppy, innocent and defenseless—not at all like the offspring of the 'king of the forest.' She glanced at the fox curled in the corner of its pen, then at the drowsing falcon, its wing immobilized.

"You know you're breaking the law?" she said.

"I don't give a damn," the doctor snapped. "They can write a thousand regulations—I'll save whatever I can. These aren't my first illegal patients, and they won't be the last."

The laws regarding wild animals had long been criticized on veterinary forums. Animal-rights groups lamented them and fought unsuccessfully for change, publicizing every case in which strict compliance caused harm. Janina didn't limit herself to vocal disapproval—she treated injured wildlife whenever necessary, using magic freely to conceal her work from outsiders. Only Piotrek and Karolina Wardecka, a married pair of journalists living above the Oxygen, had been entrusted with the secret. She knew they could be trusted. Once healed, the animals returned to the wild and no one was worse for it.

Trouble began when releasing the animal was impossible— or when someone had abandoned it. Then Janina had to turn the world upside down to find a permanent home. Usually Edi's friends helped, especially Ada Bielska and Marek Mokrzycki. Marek was particularly useful. No one in his human circle—not even his closest friends—knew who he really was, and he used his elvish charm to manipulate people. Thanks to him, homes were easily found for unwanted pets. But this time he was unavailable—he had left for a holiday in Egypt with his adopted human family and wouldn't return until the end of September.

"What will happen to the little one when he grows up?" Edi finally handed the wolf pup back to the increasingly anxious labrador, who sniffed him with relief and began to lick him vigorously.

"Hard to say. We'll see. For now he has a home and a surrogate mother, and that's all that matters." Janina sighed deeply. "It's her I worry about more. Such a trusting, gentle creature…"

"It's a pity to send her to the shelter, but I'll have to if no one comes forward."

"Uncle Fred put up notices everywhere he could."

"He did, and so what? You know this area. Countryside. And I'm not handing her over to anyone who'll keep her on a chain."

"Maybe some city folk will call. She's very pretty." Edi stroked the labrador's great head without thinking.

It was their constant worry—finding homes for all the unwanted, abandoned animals that passed through the clinic at any time of year. Never-ending work, usually difficult, often unpleasant, yet it strained their nerves less than this.

"I need an assistant for the summer, maybe longer," Janina said after a moment. "Would you be interested?"

Her niece shot her a sideways look from under her joined brows. She had once plucked the hairs bridging the base of her nose, but abandoned the habit after coming to Little Świerkowa. People claimed those brows made her look like she'd been born a shrew, but she didn't care. They were like a family crest, and she felt a certain pride in having them.

"What about Mom? Won't she raise hell? I was supposed to rest."

Dr. Batory was deftly changing the bandage on the neck of a dachshund who belonged to a vacationer from the campground by Crystal Lake. The little dog snapped, trying to bite the hand treating his wounds, but he aimed at empty air. Janina had plenty of practice dodging such 'tokens of gratitude', as she called them with dark humor.

"I'm not sure your mother is truly concerned about your rest," she said after a moment. "I've got the impression she simply doesn't want you studying veterinary medicine. I remember how furious she was when I started… She said I was disgracing the family, and the profession of a witch in general."

"But it's my life, not hers!"

Janina gave a sour smile. She examined the Caucasian shepherd dog in the largest pen, its leg cast all the way to the shoulder blade, and gave the shaggy beast a pat on the neck.

"Try to be understanding. We're from another age, and Jadwiga is… very domineering. She always has been, even when we were children. Fighting her won't be easy, though I imagine you'll manage. You're as stubborn as she is—and on top of that, quite the little spitfire. Hand me the gloves, let's examine our wild ones."

The fox was still groggy from anesthesia and let himself be examined without protest. The falcon, however, was another matter. Janina eventually had to use a touch of magic to calm him.

"In my opinion, a witch makes excellent doctor material—not only for animals," Edi declared firmly, absentmindedly checking whether any overlooked parasites still hid under the bird's feathers. When he had arrived at the clinic, he'd been battered, exhausted, and tormented by ticks and lice. The doctor had removed them, but at every check-up they had to make sure nothing had reappeared.

"No doubt," her aunt agreed. "Except it isn't our place to decide that. Your mother has a point or two, I admit, though that doesn't mean I approve of her methods." She fell silent briefly, rubbing her forehead with the back of her hand. "There was something else I meant to tell you…"

She frowned, clearly making a sincere effort to recall what had slipped her mind. A moment later she waved it off.

"Oh well… It must not be important if I've forgotten. Let's finish up and go home. Someone may call at any moment asking us to come see a four-legged patient."

"If only clients had your mobile number…"

"Then I'd never know a moment's peace. No, thank you. Things are fine the way they are."

When they stepped out of the small hospital building, a huge shadow swept suddenly over their heads. The doctor looked up, startled. There was nothing in the sky that could explain such an anomaly.

"What the devil?"

"Maybe the weather-mages are training apprentices to make clouds?" Edi suggested, pointing at a few small puffs overhead.

"No, it must've been something else. I can feel magic, but I can't pinpoint the source." Janina looked worried. "Come on— home."

Rounding the driveway, they saw someone waiting on the porch of the Spruce House, hunched on the steps. At their approach he slowly rose. What struck Edi first was how incredibly tall he was—easily over two meters—but even more startling was how massive. She saw it clearly as they came closer. Not fat, and not shaped like a bodybuilder either. Simply broad, as if carved from a huge square block. A head perched on a thick neck above shoulders worthy of a gorilla: an elongated skull covered with sleek hair, pointed ears with lobes hanging almost to the shoulders, protruding cheekbones, a long nose, close-set eyes glowing silver, and narrow lips drawn down at the corners.

"Oh, wonderful," Janina muttered despairingly. "Just what I needed. What do you want?"

"Big pain... here." The man pressed a huge hand to his stomach. His voice boomed with a metallic timbre, as if it echoed inside an iron barrel.

"Get inside before someone sees you."

Intrigued, Edi followed her aunt and the strange visitor into the examination room where Janina usually treated the animals brought to her.

"Strip to the waist," the doctor ordered briskly, pulling on her apron and gloves. "What did you eat?"

"Dinner." The man obediently removed his sweatshirt, revealing enormous arms and a broad, hairless chest. His skin had an unhealthy hue and a rough texture like a lizard's.

"At this hour I doubt it was dinner," Janina snapped. "I'm asking what, specifically."

The peculiar patient lowered his head, suddenly looking guilty.

"Well... r-rat," he muttered. Edi grimaced with revulsion.

"Oh, marvelous," sighed the doctor. "And you—stop listening in! Bring me an apomorphine[7] injection, sterile swabs, a five-mill syringe, and a puncture needle."

---

[7] Apomorphine – a drug with a strong emetic effect (despite the name, it has nothing to do with morphine).

45

"Why a puncture needle?"

"Because any other will bend and snap. And fetch the bucket—the big enamel one. We need to induce vomiting as fast as possible."

The girl obediently fetched the ampoule and supplies, then grabbed the bucket from the back room, wondering how on earth an ordinary needle could break during such a basic injection. She had never heard of anything like that.

But Janina hadn't been exaggerating. She struggled hard to get the thick needle under the patient's skin and nearly snapped it anyway. At last she managed to administer the medicine, and moments later the man erupted into the bucket like a volcano. Without delay the doctor collected samples of the stomach contents into several test tubes, adding different reagents to each.

"Mhm," she said after a while. "Sodium fluoroacetate. Lovely. Edi, bring the stomach-pump kit. Then fetch all our activated charcoal and calcium gluconate. And put on an apron—you'll need to help."

Edi hurried to gather everything, but when she stepped back into the room, she nearly dropped the lot. What she saw now she had somehow missed before: the man, kneeling forward, his back exposed, the vertebrae starkly outlined—along with a ridge running down from neck to pelvis. Thick, slightly curved spines rose and fell with his breathing.

"Auntie…?" she began, but Janina cut her off sharply:

"Later. Give me everything."

Stomach pumping is an unpleasant procedure. Animals are usually strapped down for it, or restrained[8] in metal frames in the case of cattle, or sedated—but none of that was an option now, since the doctor's patient was clearly a sentient being and could not be treated like, say, a cow. If a creature this size began to struggle, the teenage girl would never hold him. Fortunately, he behaved sensibly, and Edi's task was merely to support his head at the proper angle. When they finished, he was moved to the small room behind the office, where they laid him on two examination couches pushed together.

"Bring me another puncture needle, the thickest one," Janina told her. "I need to set up a drip, and it's going to be very difficult. And fetch the bedpan—the men's one, obviously."

"Auntie, can you *please* explain—" Edi began, but the doctor pushed her back toward the door.

---

[8] A tamer is a device made of a high-strength material, formerly made of wood, and nowadays made of metal sections, usually equipped with handles and belts enabling the restraint and immobilization of a large animal for the purpose of performing a veterinary procedure or surgery.

"He's a dragon. Happy? Now get the needle—I'll prepare the rest."

A dragon? Edi loved reading about them, and memories of every book she'd ever read sprang up at once—from Lem's *The Cyberiad* to the little-known in Poland series by Paweł Szumiło she'd recently discovered. Every author treated the subject differently. Lem claimed they were "exceptionally stupid and vile beasts", while others—like Roger Zelazny—insisted they were intelligent and civilized. Edi always preferred the latter view. As a child she had cried, Wednesday Addams–style, over a slain dragon in shining-armor tales, and Tamara[9] had needed ages to calm her. Still, she had never imagined dragons might look like *this*, though in a few stories they could assume human form—like Borch Three-Jackdaws in her beloved *Witcher*. Yet in none of them was that form so far removed from a normal human shape.

She brought her aunt the bedpan and the requested needle. Janina attached it to the prepared drip and tied a thick tourniquet[10] around the patient's arm. A vessel bulged under the rough skin a moment later.

---

[9] Tamara – housekeeper at the Gwerski house and Edi's caregiver until her parents' death (see volume I).

[10] Tourniquet – here: a rubber tube used as a bandage for blood collection, now replaced by compression straps, much more unpleasant for the patient.

"Hold his hand," she instructed.

Edi gripped the man's wrist tightly with both hands. His skin felt like a lizard's—rough and incredibly tough, as were the muscles beneath it. She didn't even try to imagine the strength he must possess. She watched her aunt's efforts, holding her breath; it was obvious how hard it was to pierce a dragon's skin and thread a needle into a vein surprisingly narrow for such a massive body, without snapping the metal. Her tongue itched to ask why Janina didn't use magic, but she wisely kept silent, saving all questions for later. Finally the doctor succeeded. She secured the insertion site with tape and tied the dragon's arm to the edge of the couch.

"That's so you don't accidentally tear the whole setup apart," she explained. "You'll need to urinate, so use this contraption." She pressed the bedpan into his free hand. "And don't you dare try to stand up, or I'll lose my temper."

"No stand," the dragon agreed meekly.

"Now something else. And you must drink all of it."

There was a great deal of powdered charcoal. Janina mixed it with distilled water until it formed a thick slurry and spooned it into his mouth, portion by portion, until he swallowed the last.

"I'll be right back. I just need to arrange someone to cover emergencies. My niece will stay with you so you don't feel abandoned."

Edi hid a grimace. She wasn't fearful by nature, but she felt uneasy around this creature—and once the door closed behind her aunt, the discomfort sharpened. Without showing it, she dragged a three-legged stool to the couches and sat down.

"You all right?" she asked, wiping the charcoal-stained corners of his mouth with a piece of gauze. He turned his remarkable silver eyes toward her.

"Better," he answered dully.

"My name is Edyta."

"Edita."

"Edyta. Though people call me Edi. And you?"

He smiled, strained but genuine.

"Koba. Thanking. You help. Not die, yes?"

"Definitely not," she assured him quickly. "My aunt is a very good doctor. I'll be one too, someday. That's my dream, you know? For now I help her. For experience. And I really like this work. I love animals—I want to help them, and dryads, and water-sprites, and all the others…" She babbled on, trying to bury the unease this enormous man still stirred in her. She didn't understand why she felt it. She'd never reacted like this around truly dangerous beings, so she puzzled over it—and felt a little annoyed with herself.

The dragon listened courteously, his pointed ear flicking now and then. He looked exhausted by all he had endured, but gradually steadied.

"You fear me," he said suddenly.

Edi fell silent.

"No, that's not—"

"I feel it. Be calm. I not hurt. I hurt no one."

Flustered, she touched his arm awkwardly, her fingers brushing the rough skin. She hadn't realized she was giving anything away—or perhaps he was simply more perceptive than his appearance suggested.

"It's just that this is my first time dealing with a dragon," she explained. "I didn't think you existed."

"Safer that way. People hate us. We hide. But must eat."

"Understandable. But why rats?"

Koba smiled.

"Tasty," he said, licking his lips with his forked tongue. "Very tasty."

"Right," Edi replied without enthusiasm. "But at least don't hunt in human settlements. Rats become resistant to poison quickly, but hawks and owls die from it when they catch them. As you see, it harms you too."

He looked ashamed.

"Understand. But be very hungry then... Edi... Turn around."

"Huh?"

"I must..."

"Oh—right, got it."

She turned on her stool. A moment later she heard the unmistakable splash behind her.

"Done."

She turned back, took the brimming bedpan, and emptied it into the bucket of stomach contents. For now the foul mixture had to wait; it contained a powerful toxin and couldn't be poured down the drain. Edi rinsed the bedpan and returned it to Koba.

"Sorry," he muttered, embarrassed.

"For what? You need to flush your kidneys, poor thing. That's what the drip is for."

The door creaked and Janina entered.

"All arranged," she said. "Run along home now, kiddo. I'll take care of our guest. And let no one disturb me."

CHAPTER III

"Dragons are very rare these days," Janina explained to her niece as they sat together on the veranda at dusk. "Or rather, to be factually correct, they are rarely seen, because no one really knows how many there are. Sometimes they appear, and then just as quickly vanish. They live their own mysterious lives somewhere unknown, probably in another dimension. Whatever it is, wherever it is, it has one drawback: there's very little food. That's why they venture into human-inhabited areas. They snatch livestock, occasionally break into slaughterhouses, but most of all, they hunt rats. That's their favorite treat."

"And rats can be poisoned."

"Yes, just like mice, which predatory birds often die from. I've told creatures like Koba to catch only rats living far from humans, but there's always some fool who can't resist a fat one from the suburbs. And then there's trouble."

"Will he be okay?" Edi asked her aunt.

"I think so. I did what I could."

For a moment, they were silent, watching the darkening sky.

"Auntie, what are dragons like?" the girl finally asked.

The doctor sighed.

"Not very intelligent in a general sense, but quite adept in a special kind of magic—the magic of elements," she replied. "Contrary to the dark legends, they are not aggressive and don't eat humans, but if cornered, they can defend themselves effectively."

"Do they breathe fire?"

"Not exactly, you silly," Janina said with a kind laugh. "How do you imagine that technically? They're protein-based creatures like us—they'd burn their mouths and tongues, if not worse. No, they use a rather clever trick, like a certain beetle, the bombardier[11] beetle."

Edi searched her memory but couldn't recall ever having heard of such an insect. She wasn't interested in entomology and didn't see the need, especially since she loved nature but had a certain prejudice against insects, some of which she was even afraid of.

"What kind of beetle is that?"

---

[11] The bombardier beetle is a species of ground beetle with a defense mechanism described by Janina.

"A little clever fellow. Frogs hunt it, so it developed an interesting strategy. When threatened, it shoots a corrosive liquid at a temperature of a hundred degrees toward its attacker."

"How is that possible?!"

"It is possible. In its abdomen, it has a sac filled with a mixture of hydrogen peroxide and hydroquinone. When threatened, it pushes this into a chamber containing enzymes: catalase and peroxidase. A strongly exothermic reaction[12] occurs, followed by a precise shot. Interestingly, this liquid never reaches boiling point inside the beetle's body, only outside."

"I hate bugs," Edi muttered in disgust. "Do dragons do the same?"

"In a way. Their sublingual glands extract phosphorus from their food and store it in throat pouches. That's why their necks are so thick. The phosphorus rests safely suspended in protective mucus. When a dragon spits it into the air, doing so at bullet-like speed, the mucus evaporates from friction, and the phosphorus ignites upon contact with air. That's the whole secret. That's more than enough to cause damage, and in the old

---

[12] Exothermic reaction – one that occurs with the release of heat.

days, it could easily turn a heavily armored knight into a roast in a baking pan."

Edi nodded, showing she understood, and her thoughts returned to the books she had read.

"You know, Auntie, a Russian writer, Pawel Szumił, wrote a really nice series about dragons," she said. "It hasn't been published in Poland yet, but a friend of mine on Facebook translated the books into Polish as a hobby. An interesting person... he's also a writer but hasn't had much luck with publishers. Maybe because he's disabled, nearly deaf, and has difficulty moving."

"That's hardly a reason!"

"I meant that's why he lacks influence. In Poland, it's not easy to convince a publisher to take on a book, especially when the author is practically unknown and writes unconventionally. You need great persuasive skill and aggressiveness, which he doesn't have. A shame. But he sent me the files, and I read them."

"Are they at least interesting?"

"Very interesting and amusing. That's not the point. This dragon, Koba, is completely different from Shumil's. Different from anyone's."

Janina smiled wearily.

"That happens. In certain matters, people like to replace knowledge with stories, especially when they don't believe in something. But what makes him so 'different'?"

"Well, the way he looks. You couldn't mistake him for a human," Edi rested her head on her aunt's shoulder. "And the way he speaks. Like someone with a mental disability—but he definitely isn't. And the fact that he even speaks! Andrzej Sapkowski wrote that it's impossible with a forked tongue."

The doctor shifted impatiently.

"That Sapkowski knows a lot. I tried reading his work and quickly gave up. A mix of rural legends, borrowings from various sources, and nonsense so absurd I don't know where he got it. Dragons do have trouble with human speech, true, but that's because of differences in brain structure, in the part responsible for semantics. They struggle to grasp human vocabulary and especially grammar, whose meaning they cannot understand. As for the tongue, yes, it's forked like a snake's, but it has an interesting property: when a dragon wants to speak, it shapes it so that it becomes similar to a human tongue. Nature is a clever trickster, my dear." She sighed deeply. "Meeting a dragon is incredibly rare, even for someone like me. They live their own lives and avoid humans whenever possible, and we, witches, respect their privacy."

"I wonder if I'll ever see Koba again," the girl whispered thoughtfully.

"I wouldn't count on it. Although, who knows…"

***

Summer was drawing to a close. Dr. Batory had already returned from her annual "job" in the mountains, where she had earned enough to pay off her outstanding bills, and together with her assistant, she took care of current matters. During harvest season, emergency calls were much fewer – not because farm animals were healthier, but because farmers simply had less time for them. As a result, in the fall, local veterinarians were overwhelmed with clients, and treating neglected animals became much more complicated.

"You know what? You're irresponsible," Jadwiga Gwerska said, greeting her sister. "Not only are you dragging this child around and burdening him with work that would be too much for a strong man, but you're also supporting idiotic ideas. She's not your daughter to make decisions for."

"I make my own decisions," Edi interrupted briskly, her face instantly puffing up like an angry parrot. "Exactly from the moment I picked up my ID card at the city hall. And even before that, my aunt respected my right to self-determination more than you did. What exactly do you want from me? For me to get married and become a housewife?"

Jadwiga looked at her with unexpected sadness.

"You're more innately Janka than me. I have no idea how that's possible, but it is. No, I don't want you to be a housewife, but rather to achieve something truly significant in life. Do you know how much someone with magical abilities can accomplish in diplomacy or economics? Do you know what you're giving up? Can you assess that? At your age and with your limited experience?"

"I no longer have magical abilities."

"Nonsense!" Jadwiga tugged at her daughter's hand and dragged her into the bathroom. "Get off those stinking clothes and get on the scales."

"What for?"

"Already!"

With a slight shudder, Edi stripped off her clothes and stepped onto the old-fashioned medical scale. Her mother deftly adjusted the weights on the swinging scale, pulled out a measuring cup, and rested its lever against the girl's head. Then she pulled out a notebook from the cabinet, a notebook Janina had kept since her niece came into her care, and shoved it under her nose.

"Look. When you arrived here, you were five feet seven (a lot for a fourteen-year-old) and weighed eighty-five pounds. And here are your measurements from before your first participation in the Summoning Ceremony. Five feet seven and a half, fifty-one pounds, and twenty-five pounds. And you haven't changed a bit since. Look at the note from before the action in which you broke the Medusa Spell—it's identical. And since then? The same. Not a bit one way or the other. I was especially careful about that. Look at your hair and nails. They're still the same length, and that doesn't mean anything to you?"

Edi stared at the entries for a moment. It was so simple, she couldn't find the words. Why hadn't she thought of it before? Maybe she was so used to not having to trim her nails that she hadn't paid attention to such a small detail. Suddenly, she remembered the conversation with Kurt, which had somehow escaped her memory. Perhaps she was supposed to forget it? Someone had made sure of that? Finally, she looked at Janina, standing in the bathroom doorway.

"Auntie?"

The doctor shrugged.

"What was I supposed to tell you? I thought you'd figure it out on your own eventually. Get in the shower now that you're naked. I want to take a bath too."

The confused girl obeyed and, wrapped in a towel, ran straight from the bathroom to her room. She pulled a long-unused e-reader out of a drawer and opened it.

"Is it possible that I haven't lost my Gift at all?" she asked.

An inscription in decorative cursive script began to form on the boards, blackened with age.

"There are exceptions to every rule. You are one of them."

"Then why don't I feel it at all?"

"The time will come, you will feel it." was the enigmatic answer.

"Are you sure I have it?"

"Without him, I'd be just a piece of wood to you. And I guess I'm not." Needless to say, this reader had a personality of its own, and an ironic one at that.

"How long will my suspension, so to speak, last?" Edi asked. "When can I return to studying magic?"

"Faster than you think. Life still has more than one surprise in store for you."

The discouraged girl closed the reader angrily. There was no point in pursuing the subject any further, because this spiritual object, though it had to answer her, did so on its own terms, and whenever it wanted, it would wriggle out of it for hours, in more or less witty ways.

So she's still a witch *in the state of being born*[13],as her aunt jokingly called it—a chemical term, she knew. She suddenly felt immense excitement and a wild joy, bordering on euphoria. She had regained something she had thought irretrievably lost. It was as if the weight that had been crushing her heart for months had suddenly melted away and vanished. It was as if she had been born again. She hurriedly put on the sweatpants she'd worn around the house and ran downstairs.

Jadwiga Gwerska sat in the living room, staring out the window, lost in clearly unhappy thoughts. For some reason, despite her stunning beauty and everyday elegance, Edi suddenly seemed so lonely and unhappy that the girl ran to her and threw her arms around her neck.

"I love you, Mom," she whispered in her ear.

Jadwiga returned her hug tightly and warmly, and suddenly tears welled up in her eyes.

"Do you know that's the first time you've told me this since I got here?"

"I'm sorry," Edi said, feeling guilty and kissing her cheek. "So much has happened."

---

[13]In statu nascendi – literally "in the process of being created" (Latin).

"I know, and I've been a bit bossy at times. You know, you're my only child, and I want you to succeed so badly."

"And that's why you took my papers from the dean's office? Sorry, Mom, it slipped my mind."

"It doesn't matter, darling," Jadwiga wiped her wet eyes and smiled. "Now I can tell you what I really meant. You see... You had a meeting with... you know who. Have you read 'The Master and Margarita'?"

"Yes, superficially."

"Well, you know how this can end. The human mind is too weak and can easily collapse in such an encounter. I didn't want to risk it... I had to observe you to make sure you weren't hurt."

"So, did I just sneeze?" Edi almost laughed. "My high school friends thought I was a freak anyway. They'd call out to me in the hallways, 'Oh, here comes Wednesday Addams!' They wouldn't even realize anything had changed."

"If that happened, I'd rather one of us noticed than a stranger, especially at the university. We could have done something about it before it spread and gotten you back to some sort of order. We have our methods."

The young girl sat down on the sofa next to her mother and looked out the window with her for a while.

"Nothing really happened to me," she finally said. "Is that so strange?"

"Not for a witch. However, initially it was unclear what would happen to you. If you had truly become an ordinary person, things might have been different. He exerts an incredibly strong influence on the mind; the average "human" couldn't withstand such pressure."

Edi remembered something.

"Mom, did Tamara Sukhotina know who you were? And who I might be?"

Mrs. Gwerska nodded.

"Tamara is a well-known whisperer in Ukraine, very wise and a friend of our family. I brought her in so you would have a guardian who would be able to react to any situation and deal with any danger. This may surprise you now, even outrage you, but from the beginning, I wanted the Dar to never manifest within you. I even asked Tamara to give you a blocker when you were growing up. I don't even know if she did."

"She did. It's that forked coral on the chain, right? I still have it, in my drawer."

"You were supposed to wear it around your neck, but I guess you didn't."

65

Edi grimaced mischievously and tried unsuccessfully to feign remorse.

"No. But that's probably a good thing, right?"

Jadwiga did not answer immediately.

"Everything has its price," she finally sighed. "I wanted to spare you the suffering we share. However, if you've already chosen... well, too bad. I have to agree to this, or rather, accept it as a fait accompli."

"And you will teach me like an aunt?"

Gwerska smiled sadly.

"Actually... Why not?"

Janina entered the living room, wrapped in a dressing gown and smelling of bath salts.

"Oh, you two finally got along? Great," she patted Edi on the back with satisfaction and went to change. A moment later, she returned in a light, house dress. "So, girls, what are we having for dinner?"

Her sister waved her hand.

"I don't feel like cooking. Let's order pizza like we're a normal family."

"Oh yes, I could use some chow!" Edi clapped her hands. "Auntie, I'll have a Hawaiian with double Parmesan! And barbecue wings with that! A large Pepsi Zero and sweet rolls with raspberries!"

"A real killer for the liver. But once in a while won't hurt. You, Jadzia?"

"Margherita, diablo sauce, apple calzone and Lipton Ice Tea lemon."

"I think I'll take the same. Fred!"

"What's up, little sister?" Janina and Jadwiga's brother, not entirely happy, peered out from his room, which was adjacent to the living room. "I'm playing Twister with Alinka."

"Twister with a nymph? You're already lying at the beginning; they're as flexible as young willow branches. Make yourself useful. Take your scooter and bring us a pizza. I'll write down which ones to buy so you forget." The doctor took her notebook with a pen attached.

Alinka ran out of the room, clapping her hands and shaking her disheveled hair, from which all the pins had fallen out during the game.

"I'll come with you! I'll help carry the groceries!" she exclaimed. She loved riding her scooter.

"Okay, fine," Fred sighed demonstratively, taking the slip of paper and the money. "You treat me like an errand boy."

"Are you good at anything else, you lazy idiot? Go away".

The offended man went out into the hall, from where after a while he could be heard mumbling something angrily and opening the door with a bang, after which he suddenly fell silent.

"Hey, ladies, we have a guest!" he called after a moment. "And what a guest! And let the current caress me..."

CHAPTER IV

A slow, unhurried figure was making her way toward the veranda: a short, very slender woman of indeterminate age. She wore an old-fashioned ankle-length skirt and a lace-trimmed blouse, her hair arranged in a low bun at the nape of her neck, vaguely reminiscent of old portraits of society ladies. As she walked, she leaned slightly on a straight cane topped with a carved handle, which created a peculiar impression, for she did not appear to have any difficulty moving without it. On the contrary. Only by looking closely could one notice that she stepped a bit more cautiously on her right leg.

"Who is that?" Edi asked her aunt, looking curious.

"Emilia Gotsary," the doctor replied, stunned. "The senior of our family. I haven't heard of her for what must be a hundred years, and besides, she was never very sociable, not to mention her position…"

"What position?"

"She is the Grand Librarian," Janina added, seeing the girl's expression. "I'll explain later what that title really means."

They stood at the doorway, watching the woman approach. When she stepped onto the veranda, they moved aside to allow her to cross the threshold of the house unimpeded, which she did with the calm dignity of a monarch, everywhere acting as if she were at home.

Up close, Emilia Gotsary did not look like a witch, nor particularly old. She had fair, almost porcelain-like skin, black eyes with a piercing gaze, delicate features befitting a grand lady, and small, very red lips. She didn't seem elderly, though slightly sagging cheeks and faint crow's feet at her temples suggested she was no longer in her first youth. Her smoothly combed black hair bore discreet traces of gray. Yet her slender hands were exquisite—smooth, like sculpted ivory, long fingers ending in oval nails, naturally pink and polished to a silky shine. Edi could admire them at leisure, for the newly met relative, having seated herself in a chair, placed her hands on her knees, in accordance with the social etiquette of a bygone era.

"What will the cousin have to drink?" Jadwiga asked respectfully.

"Cardamom coffee," Emilia replied calmly. "Only real sugar, please. No sweeteners or substitutes."

After a moment, a porcelain coffee pot, a sugar bowl with tongs, cups, and a plate of pastries appeared on a seldom-used coffee table, all from Doctor Batory's finest service, usually kept locked in the cupboard. The old, hand-painted Chinese porcelain was too valuable to be used except on truly rare occasions, and Edi had never seen it before. Hesitantly, she took a cup with thin, semi-transparent walls, decorated with intricate ornaments. She watched, enchanted, as their guest gracefully lifted the delicate vessel to her lips, took a sip, and then dabbed her mouth with a lace handkerchief.

The others barely dared to sit, as if the English queen herself had visited. Even usually restless Alinka crouched quietly in a corner, not daring to move. Only Popo ignored the presence of the dignified guest, loudly purring on his pillow by the windowsill, lazily licking his paws.

"I think she wants to say something cutting right away, but has decided to wait. This could be interesting," Edi thought.

"What does the cousin want from my daughter?" Jadwiga asked coldly. She did not appreciate the tone of the unexpected visitor.

"She is only 'your daughter,'" Emilia tapped her cane lightly on the floor to emphasize her words. "The youngest descendant of our family. An extraordinarily talented child, whom you are trying to waste, which, frankly, is not surprising. There have always been difficulties with the Batorys of both genders. You are unpredictable and headstrong, preventing your talents from developing as they should."

"That's an exaggeration, cousin," protested Janina, offended. "We both manage perfectly well."

"I have a different opinion. But that's irrelevant now. Stefan is dead, Fred turned out to be a dry branch, and the two of you will learn nothing more." Emilia spoke calmly, yet in a way that no one dared to interrupt. "I am here to take over Edyta's care. From now on, I will teach her and ensure she develops properly."

Her words sounded sharp and categorical.

"Zywia also thought that would be best," Fred said after she finished, gently picking up one of the cream pastries with the sugar tongs. "But we are not talking about a canary in a cage, nor do we live in the Middle Ages. The girl has the right to decide for herself, and as far as I know, she does not consent to such changes in her life."

"Of course not!" the girl huffed angrily.

Emilia cast her a prolonged gaze that sent shivers down Edi's spine. She realized that her relative was trying to impose her will, and she resisted with all her strength. She had never fought such an unusual battle, entirely focused on the psyche. Time seemed to stand still, the pressure mounting. Edi felt as if she were caught in pincers from which she could not escape, yet she refused to capitulate. When she could no longer catch her breath, the pressure of the encroaching power suddenly vanished so abruptly that she fell off the chair in surprise.

"You are indeed very strong," Emilia said calmly. "And stubborn as a mule, which, incidentally, is a family trait. Listen to me carefully now. Until last century, young people listened to their elders, and it worked well for everyone. Today, the young listen only to themselves, despise anyone older (if they have a different opinion, of course), and disrupt the world order. Powerful political forces take advantage of their blindness, leading naive puppies wherever they want. In our world, this is unacceptable." She tapped her cane on the floor for emphasis. "That is why witches and magicians still exist. If such a puppyocracy as now exists among humans prevailed among us, it would be the end of us."

"I don't believe that at all!" Edi protested, struggling to get up from the floor. She felt as if she had just finished a marathon, battered by a herd of cattle at the finish line. "No one should be discriminated against just for being young. Young people have their own judgment."

"Yet to devalue someone simply for being older, to call them a 'fossil' or a 'moher,' and claim they should be locked away somewhere, is perfectly fine, right? Don't you see everything is upside down, and it's impossible to function like that for long?"

Emilia sighed sadly and shook her head. "You say they have judgment? Whoever truly has it listens to the advice of experienced people. Let me give you an example: two climbers are ascending Mount Everest. They have visual and audio communication via Bluetooth. One, very high up, tells the other, 'Change your route, the rock you're climbing may collapse.' The second replies indignantly, 'You won't tell me what to do, I know what I'm doing, I have my own judgment.' Who do you think he will blame when he falls?"

Edi rubbed her bruised elbow gloomily and said nothing.

"Honorable cousin, we all understand your intentions here," Jadwiga began. "We also do not intend to oppose your authority. But times have truly changed, and my daughter is a special case."

"So special that you hired a woman to block her Gift before it had a chance to manifest."

"Perhaps," Gwerska admitted. "But it didn't work. Now it's about what comes next. Of course, you could teach her, but nothing will come of it if she is unwilling. You cannot immediately position yourself as her enemy."

Emilia raised her eyebrows, forming a swallows-shaped mark typical of women in her family.

"I am not doing that."

"That's what you think. Today's children are really different from the old times and cannot stand being treated from above. A little diplomacy won't hurt if you really want to achieve something. Edi is no exception. And in this little struggle of strength, you could have hurt her."

The elderly lady placed a pastry on a small plate and began to eat it slowly and elegantly with a teaspoon. Janina refilled her coffee and offered the sugar bowl.

The rest of the group finally decided to take a drink as well— earlier, nervousness had kept them from touching either the beverage or the sweets. Even Edi now allowed herself a sip of coffee, though she usually avoided it. Her heart was still racing, and she felt utterly exhausted.

"May I ask something?" Fred spoke up again, not waiting for permission to continue. "If I understand correctly, dear cousin, you've been observing us for quite some time. Up close?"

Emilia raised her penetrating eyes to him.

"Is that important?" she asked.

"I'm just curious whether you went to the trouble of coming from the ends of the earth, or perhaps you just live nearby. It's interesting, since no one has heard of you for a very long time. Finn Bergstrand tried to find you when Janka was kidnapped and couldn't find a trace—and he's not just any magician, but a sixth-level qualified wizard. Where have you been hiding that someone so experienced and powerful could not locate you?"

"At the House on the Rocks!" Alinka squeaked from her corner. Everyone present, surprised, looked at her in astonishment. They had almost forgotten she was there during the conversation.

The older lady smiled approvingly.

"Stop joking!" Janina shouted. "Since when has the cousin lived there?"

"More or less for half a century."

"I don't believe it!"

"Yet, my dear," Emilia took another sip of her coffee. "It's a very good location. The building is listed as a historic monument, ownership is unclear, plus a touch of magic…"

"A touch of magic?" Jadwiga snorted. "The cousin has deceived not only people but everyone in general. I didn't even know such a thing was possible."

"If you devoted more time to study and less to coquetry, you might have guessed," the Grand Librarian twisted her lips into a sardonic smile and added. "I jest, of course. It's no accident that I am who I am. I've been studying magic for five hundred fifty-three years, which means I accumulate knowledge instead of practicing actively like you. Which also means I can use every scrap of it for my own purposes. Every single one. Some of them would make your eyes pop out." She looked at Edi. "And some of that could be yours, little one. Whatever you choose. But you must be fully aware of what you are giving up or accepting."

The girl stopped massaging her injured elbow and tried for a moment to adopt the most blasé expression she could muster. It didn't really work. The prospects seemed far too tempting.

"But I don't want to move anywhere!" she immediately objected.

Emilia smiled again, this time more gently and with understanding.

"You don't have to. I enjoy peace and have no desire to live daily with a rebellious child. For now, having a young terminator is enough of a challenge, but one day I must pass the baton to a suitable successor, or at least share the responsibilities. We, too, age, unfortunately, and the time comes when it begins to weigh on us. And I... had certain problems that adversely affected my health." She pressed her hand on the carved handle of her cane. "Listen, Edyta: you thought you had lost your Gift. Now you know that's not true. I don't believe you intend to reject it, as your uncle Stefan did long ago."

"Because I won't. I want to become a full-fledged witch ever since I learned it was possible. Aunt Janina can confirm that." Edi looked at the doctor, seeking approval.

"Then you need proper education, and you need it immediately. Untaught Power, if not blocked in some way, can degenerate or grow uncontrollably, leading sooner or later to disaster. Janeczka tried to teach you, and credit to her for that, because she gave you the necessary basics. Rajmund Ciernik also did what he could—the problem is, he could only do so much. He doesn't yet have sufficient experience to teach anyone, but in the end, it's better than nothing. At least he gave you part of the essential theory, so you are not completely green today."

"And can I still continue being Aunt Janina's assistant at the clinic at the same time?"

"Why not? But learning in accordance with your Gift is at least equally important. And don't forget, your personal safety is very much in question."

"Ehhh!" the girl exclaimed in surprise. "Why? Has Janusz Mokrzycki appeared again? Have the symbiotes gathered?"

Feeling her appetite and confidence return, she took a pastry and was surprised by its flavor. Extraordinary, even overwhelming, it surpassed anything she had ever tasted. These were no ordinary cookies. Without asking anyone, she took three from the plate onto a small dish and brought them to Alinka, who was still cowering in the corner, too shy to approach the table in the presence of such a dignified guest.

"Here, you've never tasted anything like this in your life," she said, handing the plate to the nymph.

"Edi!" her mother scolded desperately, then turned to the older lady, who stirred her coffee with an unflinching expression. "I apologize for her. The cousin understands; today's youth…"

Emilia smiled.

"As far back as I can remember, youth has always been 'today's youth.' Spoiled, ill-mannered, foolish, disrespectful, hopeless. And in a hundred or two hundred years, it will be the same." She put the teaspoon down on the saucer. "Today's problem is that with social media, which didn't exist before, we have a true puppyocracy, and it seems no one dares to rein in the noisy brats. Some groups even benefit from this, because young people are easily manipulated into becoming fervent promoters of the craziest and most harmful ideas. In fact, to the point of dying for them! This cannot end well. There have been precedents in past centuries, though the internet did not exist then."

"Like what?" Edi bristled. She didn't feel particularly connected to her peers, yet the way the matter was framed immediately provoked strong opposition in her.

Unperturbed, Emilia recited:

Ah, I remember the times when French fashion
First visited our Fatherland!
When suddenly young masters from foreign lands
Invaded us in hordes worse than the Nogai,
Persecuting God, ancestors' faith,
Laws and customs, even old dresses
It was pitiful to see yellowed youths,
Talking through their noses, sometimes without noses,
Equipped with pamphlets and various newspapers,
Proclaiming new faiths, laws, and toilets.
That rabble had great power over minds;
For when God sends punishment on a nation,
He first takes away reason from its citizens.
And so the wiser dared not oppose the novices,
The whole nation feared them like the plague,
Feeling the seed of disease within themselves;
Fashionable youths were scolded, yet emulated;
Faith, language, laws, and dress were changed.
It was a masquerade, carnival revelry,

After which came the great fast—slavery![14]

"Come on! That's just poetic metaphor!" the girl protested. "Everything has to be the fault of young people? Isn't that exaggeration? We're not that bad! It's today's youth who raised awareness of the need to protect the planet and fight for it. Greta Thunberg…"

She stopped, daunted by the older lady's gaze.

"I'm not saying you're bad. Your enthusiasm and fresh perspective are invaluable, but they must be balanced by the wisdom and experience of elders. There used to be a saying: 'A young heart in a gray head is the nation's reason.' Now it's the opposite, and the whole world is going mad." Emilia spoke calmly, her tone dignified yet lowered. "Greta Thunberg, whom you were kind enough to mention, is merely a puppet animated by seasoned businessmen. Take the trouble to examine her life path, including family connections, and you'll see it for yourself. So-called 'ecologism'—not to be confused with real ecology—is an excellent machine for making money and eliminating competition through the hands of brainwashed youth. I am amazed people still don't see it; it's as clear as day."

---

[14] "Pan Tadeusz", Adam Mickiewicz, Book I.

"Some do see it," Fred remarked. "But they are politically and socially suppressed. Enemies of the planet, you understand, cousin?"

"It's just a trend that will pass, and one day it will be mocked, like corsets and powdered wigs today. Darling, may I have some cream for my coffee?" the Grand Librarian addressed Janina. The doctor hastily handed her a small silver pitcher, surely not previously on the table.

"But this trend allows ruthless people to dominate entire societies. There's little we can do about that, and I'm not here to debate ecology. This is about the child."

Edi stamped her foot in anger and swallowed the rest of the pastry in one go, so she wouldn't have to speak with her mouth full.

"I'm not a child!" she shouted.

"By reacting this way, you prove that you still are. But that's irrelevant," Emilia said, hardly ever losing her composure. "What matters is something else."

"Yes, yes!" the rebellious girl interrupted, stamping again. "That I'm the last hope of the family and a gift to the world, and soooo much depends on me. So much that I have no say in it whatsoever!"

"Nonsense," the older lady was clearly amused. "What is running through that poor little head of yours?"

Edi blushed.

"Well, because in a movie or a book, it would be like that…" she mumbled, embarrassed.

Emilia smiled indulgently, watching her.

"You're probably right, it would. At your age, you're entitled to think you are some kind of chosen one, since you broke the Medusa Spell—not without help from experienced mages, mind you—befriended the Titans, and even the Dark Lord himself took an interest in you… But you could use a bit of common sense. I must disappoint you. You are not so much the best among young talent, as practically the only one in Poland suitable for any training at all. We have no choice today, my dear. There are many young people with the Gift, but those worth starting work with can be counted on the fingers of one hand. Above all, a lack of belief in any magic eliminates candidates immediately; moreover, the pervasive propaganda of hedonism disrupts things terribly. And most of them now have tattoos, since it's so fashionable."

Edi wrinkled her nose. Many of her classmates "got" tattoos as soon as their parents allowed it, or once they turned eighteen and no longer needed anyone's consent. Indeed, the trend was spreading widely. Initially, small, discreet designs on living skin were replaced by full-scale images, sometimes executed with great artistry, but always with a flair bordering on kitsch. Older people were succumbing to this trend as well—representatives of various professions, even teachers, doctors, and civil servants. Young Gwerska didn't see anything wrong with it, although she had never considered getting tattooed a pinnacle of her dreams, even during her goth phase.

"Aunt Janina told me that witches aren't allowed tattoos, but she didn't explain why."

"Too bad. Fortunately, you resisted that wretched trend. You see, this is not merely body art—it is very powerful blocking magic, known since the time of primitive humans. Knowing its secrets allows you to achieve various effects, from relieving chronic pain to protection against even strong enchantments. A common feature of all tattoos is the weakening, even outright extinguishing, of magical abilities, which contemporary tattoo artists, of course, have no idea about. Now you understand why we can hardly afford to be picky today, right?"

It was hard not to understand. Emilia Gocsary had a gift for explaining complex matters clearly and choosing her words carefully. Yet Edi had mixed feelings. She was used to thinking she was somehow special. It was a weakness even the most accomplished people succumbed to, let alone a teenage student. Yet she now turned out to be "the best" in the same sense as a somewhat competent runner among talented athletes with broken legs. That realization was not pleasant.

"I guess I'm worth something if you went to all this trouble to come here," she finally muttered.

"Absolutely. And just call me 'aunt.' Great-great-great-aunt would be far too pretentious." Emilia smiled. She must have had a great sense of humor, carefully concealed. "Perhaps I expressed myself imprecisely, which led to misunderstanding. In a sense, you are rare, due to your multiplied talent. That has never been common throughout history, though it has occurred occasionally. A good example is Count Saint Germain. That name probably doesn't ring a bell?"

The contrite girl shook her head.

"That's all right. You don't need to know everything. So, regardless, you are exceptional, and if you weren't, Wo… well, you know who, wouldn't have noticed you. That alone says a lot. Just to be clear: this is not a reason to be conceited, but a motivation to work, because even the greatest gifts can be wasted if not developed at the right pace. Jadzia did the right thing by delaying your studies for now," she glanced at Edi's mother, who didn't look particularly pleased with the compliment. "Don't make that face, my dear."

"It wasn't for that reason that I did it."

"And I will still study veterinary medicine, and that's nobody's business," Edi added rebelliously.

"Of course, darling. Calm down, Jadzia. I know you didn't want your daughter to follow in your footsteps, but it's inevitable, since even breaking the Medusa Spell didn't harm her Gift. Although," she frowned briefly, "we know very little about that spell. It is older than humanity, but extremely rarely used. Usually, to turn someone to stone—or rather trap them in a stone shell—the Binding Curse is sufficient. Depending on the components used, it can suspend someone in time, meaning they would need no oxygen, water, or food for any length of time, or it can kill. The Medusa Spell is much more intricate and mysterious. Even I, the Grand Librarian, Keeper of Knowledge, know almost nothing about it. So in truth, we don't really know what breaking it does to a person with the Gift."

"Rajmund said those stones sucked out the power like a sponge. That must be why…" Edi scratched her head, trying to recall what she felt touching the huge boulders. "But they didn't suck me dry. In any case, I didn't feel anything like that."

"You see. All right," Emilia leaned back, adjusting the lace cuff, and glanced at the tiny gold watch on her left wrist. "I must go. Today is Saturday, so I expect you at my house at eight on Monday morning. Take this."

She pulled a rough purple stone from her bag.

"What's this?"

"Raw amethyst, if you mean what kind of crystal. But also a so-called contractor. Touch it to the door before opening it, unless you want unpleasant experiences." The Grand Librarian neatly folded the napkin and rose, supporting herself with the cane. "No need to see me out—I know the way."

CHAPTER V

"So, what about that pizza?" Edi asked after a long silence, during which everyone had exchanged awkward glances, unsure what to say.

"Pizza?" Janina exploded, shaken. "Pizza?! You're thinking about pizza now?!"

"Well? I'm hungry."

"Do you even realize who you just met?!"

The girl shrugged and pouted.

"Yes. A very annoying old boomer who sticks her nose in everyone's business. Uncle, if you're broke, I'll give you money, but go to the pizzeria already," she said to Fred. "Unless I'm supposed to go, in which case hand me the keys."

"I'm going, I'm going, you pesky girl. Come on, Alina."

The nymph leapt up from the floor and happily ran after Fred.

"Don't use teen slang around us, okay?" sighed Jadwiga. "You don't even realize how irritating that is. You didn't used to do it."

"True." Edi admitted, somewhat embarrassed. She had never liked or used trendy terms like "sigma," "yampnig," or "pulling a fast one," which often led her schoolmates to consider her a "hopeless stiff." It didn't bother her; she was discovering a world her peers had no idea existed and seeing things they overlooked. When she lost—or thought she had lost—her magical abilities, she found herself in a kind of emotional vacuum. She tried to be more like her classmates, changed her image and manner of speaking, attended parties and concerts, and even went twice to a Fantasy Convention with the band "Rats," but she still felt it was too late to integrate. Before everything came to light, she felt desperately alone.

"Mom, now I remember that right after all that Medusa Spell fiasco, Kurt told me that I actually hadn't lost my Gift, and then I fell asleep," she said to Jadwiga. "Why didn't I remember that when I woke up?"

Her mother smiled sadly.

"Sometimes it's better that way. I had hoped I could make you a normal teenager. That you could… just live. Unfortunately, it turned out to be beyond my powers. Or maybe, for objective reasons, it simply couldn't work."

Edi nodded, full of doubt. She still couldn't decipher her mother and her motives.

"And this great-great-grandmother Emilia... what kind of character is she? Where did she come from?"

Janina stood and pulled from the closet an album bound in embossed leather. She opened it to a page and showed her niece a series of images—pencil sketches, oil portraits, and faded daguerreotypes. All depicted Emilia Gocsary in various hairstyles and outfits.

"She is currently the oldest living member of our family," she said. "Our mother, your grandmother, used to say that of all of us, she received the most gifts. 'Of us,' meaning the entire family, because in reality, Emilia is not our great-grandmother but a relative in the third line. However, she took care of me, Jadzia, Stefan, and Fred when we were left alone. We owe her a relatively safe childhood and careful education... basically everything. She cared for us until we became independent."

"I've already heard about Stefan. It even amused me a bit... Stefan Batory, like the king of Poland... What really happened to him?"

Janina grew solemn.

"He rejected his Gift. Renounced it and joined the seminary. He became a priest. It wasn't easy for him, because someone who hardly ages is always suspicious, and even more so in a clerical environment… Fortunately, he had a clear head, and we were with him, so from time to time he changed surroundings, and we went with him. Family sticks together. It required a lot of cunning, forging documents, even a bit of magic—we helped him a little. His final post was in Warsaw, at the Orionist parish, and that's how the four of us ended up in Poland, with which we were, moreover, bound by blood."

"He didn't age at all?"

"I said 'almost.' When one doesn't use the Gift, it slowly fades, and then old age and death eventually arrive, just like with ordinary people. Stefek knew that, but he stubbornly held to his choice, even when, after the fall of the Warsaw Uprising, he ended up in a concentration camp. Even in such a terrible place, he remained true to his principles and helped others as much as he could."

"The parishioners and students adored him," Jadwiga added nostalgically. "Look, that's him."

The photograph showed a curly-haired brunette with strong, striking features, an elongated face, and fiery eyes.

"What a hunk. Sharp," Edi said appreciatively.

"Yes. Similar to your father, your grandfather," Jadwiga smiled, though tears welled in her eyes. "He was a wonderful man. And he could have been an excellent mage. Emilia never accepted his choice. She cut off contact with us then, and we didn't hear from her for a long time. Later, bits of news reached us as communication technologies developed. Magical means were blocked, scientific ones weren't. We learned second-hand that, because of her abilities, she had been sent to train under the then Grand Librarian."

"Ah, yes! Who is this Librarian in your... I mean, our world?"

"She is, in other words, the Keeper of Knowledge," Janina explained. "Knowledge intended for witches. For mages, there is the Grand Librarian, the Keeper. And in fact, they always work hand in hand. When they decide to relocate, their headquarters, called the Watchtower, travels wherever they wish, which is important, because it's a huge building."

Edi's face reflected disbelief.

"And now it's somewhere here?" she asked skeptically.

"Absolutely, since Emilia is here. Only very few people see it. You can probably understand why."

"Cool." The girl shook her head and began flipping through the album, looking at the photographs, portraits, and sketches. She tapped a page with her finger. "And who's this one?"

Janina looked over her shoulder at a photocopy of a primitive drawing from an old book.

"Show a little more respect, young lady. You're looking at our ancestor."

"What do you mean?"

"She is our matrilineal forebear, supposedly. Wife of Piast, about whom little is said, all attention focused on her husband—the incompetent woodcutter—and the equally useless son, who needed supernatural help to accomplish anything at all. Meanwhile, she also had daughters, whom the chronicles do not mention, to whom she passed the Gift, received directly from one of the pre-Slavic deities. It would be hard to prove now, but oral tradition says that's how it was."

"No way. What else will I find out…" Edi giggled, her mood fully restored, especially as she saw Kurt's horned head peering through the window. "Hey, what are you doing looking through the glass? Come in!"

Jadwiga sighed in despair but said nothing.

Anyone who knew Edyta Gwerska knew how much she loved animals and that she feared no living creature. As she jokingly said, even humans. Yet when she opened a door marked "Historical Monument under Ministry of Culture Supervision," she literally jumped back. Behind it lay a completely ruined interior, where rats the size of cats and hundreds, if not thousands, of cockroaches scurried everywhere. The stench of mildew, garbage, and excrement hit her. She had not expected this. From the outside, the house looked fairly neat; the glass in the small shutters shone cleanly, though the thick curtains inside obscured the view. Anyone entering would have been equally shocked.

Stepping back from the threshold, Edi trembled for a moment before remembering the crystal hidden in her pocket.

"I'm an idiot," she muttered to herself.

She pulled out the stone, closed the door, and solemnly touched it with the amethyst before reopening it.

"Now, that I understand."

Before her stretched a tall, arched palace-style hallway. A dark red carpet lay on the floor, crystal chandeliers hung from the ceiling, and rows of enormous portraits lined both sides. Hesitantly, Edi stepped onto the carpet, and the house door closed behind her with a soft click. She shuddered again, nervously scanning for unpleasant creatures—but of course, there were none. No wonder anyone entering the House-on-the-Rocks quickly fled and never returned. Creating such a perfect, lasting illusion must have been a huge challenge.

Reaching a fork in the corridor, she hesitated on which way to go. As she looked around, a hidden door suddenly opened in one of the walls. She hadn't exactly not seen it before—she simply hadn't recognized it. Each portrait was, in fact, a sealed entrance to further rooms. Clever, she thought.

From the open room emerged a tall, bony man in a dark outfit vaguely reminiscent of some cosplay. Edi couldn't place its era—it was definitely not modern, nor did it remind her of any specific historical period. The man looked at her with a strange smile on his thin, pale, semi-translucent face, starkly contrasted by abundant black hair and anthracite eyes. Neither young nor old, he seemed starved and exhausted. Unexpectedly, he extended a long, thin hand, his fingers thickened at the joints with curved nails.

"Tukuy imapas ñuqapaq[15]," he whispered voraciously, showing sharp teeth. "Suñay[16]—"

"Hey, keep your hands to yourself!" young Gwerska shouted, jumping back. "Or I'll punch you so hard you'll hit the wall!"

The man seemed surprised by her reaction and clearly did not understand her words. He stepped forward, hesitated.

"Emilly paymi noqaman kachamurqasunki?[17]" he asked.

The entrance doors creaked, opened, and closed.

---

[15] All for me (Quechua).
[16] Gift (Quechua).
[17] Did Emilly send you to me? (Quechua).

"What's going on now?" came the voice of the Grand Librarian. "Thak kay, Araña! Payqa primoymi, estudianteymi. Payqa mana llamiy atina, yuyariy.[18]"

The man lowered his head in submission.

"Yarqasqañam kachkani, Hatun Guardia[19]."

"Cuartoykiman riy. Pisi tiempollamantan mikhunaykipaq chayanki.[20]"

"What language is that?" Edi asked, astonished, as the clearly distressed man walked away.

"Quechua," Emilia replied. "Araña comes from Latin America, from Peru. He speaks no other language except his native one and a bit of Spanish. Difficult to communicate with."

She moved further into the hallway, Edi following. She felt a mix of surprise and disappointment when she was led into an entirely normal-looking playroom.

"Wait here a moment," Emilia said, placing shopping bags on the table. "I'll just bring Araña something to eat and be right back."

---

[18] Calm down, spider. She's my cousin and student. She's untouchable, remember (Quechua).

[19] I'm hungry, Great Caretaker (Quechua).

[20] Go to your room. You'll be able to eat soon (Quechua).

Edi looked at the cheap plastic supermarket bags. They contained ordinary items: bread, vegetables, eggs, milk… She realized that her older relative looked different today than during her visit to Jodełka. More like a regular, not very young woman, dealing with everyday problems like anyone else. The disguise was understandable, though slightly disappointing, as if it reduced an aristocrat to the role of a servant.

"Who's this Araña?" she asked. "A vampire? Nice teeth."

Emilia grimaced slightly.

"Not exactly," she said hesitantly. "Or rather, not entirely. He's a pishtaco."

"What? Never heard of that."

"An endemic species of strix. It feeds on human fat, not blood. Found only in Peru and Bolivia." She paused, watching the young girl's wide eyes and dropped jaw. She sighed. "Let's treat this as your first lesson, because I see you're intrigued by this unpleasant creature. Here's the story: ethnologists link pishtacos to the practices of 16th-century conquistadors, who sometimes rendered fat from the bodies of killed Indians to grease muskets…"

"Oh God… That's horrible!"

"At the very least, not pleasant. Conquistadors were not known for moral behavior—even by the standards of their time, they were monsters. On the other hand, they simply didn't regard the Indians as human, and, considering Andean religious practices, as devilspawn. It's not entirely incomprehensible in context. In any case, ethnologists are wrong, because pishtacos are much older than the Conquest. They are extremely rare, so it's no wonder you hadn't heard of them. Today they have a paradise on Earth, with the global obesity epidemic, but once it was very hard to find food, so they mainly attacked the elites. Before the Spanish invasion, they were truly feared."

Almost imperceptibly during this speech, Emilia's simple clothing, from a cheap thrift store, transformed into a form-fitting navy gown with a standing collar and long sleeves, and her hair styled itself into an elaborate coiffure. From a weary, ordinary woman, effortlessly and without magical artifacts, the Grand Librarian became a mature lady of high society, a stern mentor with impeccable manners.

"How did this Araña end up with you, Aunt?" Edi asked, admiring her. Such a transformation, even Janina, who did strange things, probably couldn't achieve without help from words and gestures.

Emilia waved a hand dismissively.

"The Watchtower was in Bolivia at the time," she explained. "One day he wandered in and stayed."

"Wandered in? Like a puppy?"

"Exactly. I took pity on him. A hopeless case, one of those who crossed the 'Captain Nemo point.'"

"What do you mean?" A cup of strong tea, a sugar bowl, and a plate of pastries suddenly appeared in front of Edi. She drank mechanically and bit into a delicious éclair, eyes never leaving her new aunt.

"If you read more, you'd know what I mean," the Librarian said sharply. "Or you'd guess. '20,000 Leagues Under the Sea,' Jules Verne." A thick book appeared in her hands; she flipped several pages and began reading aloud. "The day the Nautilus first submerged, the world ended for me. That day I bought the last volumes, the last pamphlets, the last newspapers; from that day onward, humanity created and wrote nothing new for me."

She closed the book, which—obedient to her will—vanished, presumably returning to its place in the library.

"I think I understand," Edi said slowly, taking another bite of her pastry. "Someone who passes that point becomes unable to accept new solutions."

"Not only that. They stop understanding the world moving forward as if without them. This is also one of the attributes of human old age—not in every case, but in many. At some point, everything new ceases to exist for the aging person: new books, new music, new movies, new fashions, even new words. They can only enjoy what existed in the past. For long-lived beings, it takes a far more dramatic form and inevitably leads to misery. Mages and witches are in a privileged position here; it's easier for them to maintain a certain flexibility, allowing them to adapt to changes. Non-human entities are another story, but vampires, striges, and pishtacos, as you say today, are out of luck."

"Why?"

"Because, in truth, they are still human—at least mentally and emotionally. This awaits all of them sooner or later. Unless they encounter Hunters early enough."

"That's awful! Does that mean Uncle Fred too…?"

"All indications suggest so. But for now, he's holding on, right? The Batory genes are exceptional; perhaps this misfortune can be postponed. Or maybe you will discover some remedy." She leaned toward her. "Because magic is a science, child. Just like any other science. It doesn't stand still—it's dynamic. And it couldn't be otherwise."

Edi looked up at Emilia.

"Aunt Janina told me there are no magical universities."

"Because there aren't. But the science itself exists… only its mode is individual. It can't be any other way, because the teacher must devote their full attention to a single student and cannot be distracted by others. Returning to Araña, I've explained to him who you are, and you don't need to fear him."

"I'm not afraid," Edi sighed. "What kind of name is Araña? Is it indigenous?"

The Grand Librarian shook her head. She picked up a cup that had appeared from nowhere on the table and sipped lightly from it.

"It's not actually a name," she replied. "And that's not what he calls himself."

"What does he call himself?"

"I have no idea. He doesn't either. He doesn't remember. He is very old, even for his species, and he crossed the Nemo point. That causes exactly these kinds of problems. Araña means 'spider' in Quechua. I named him that because I eventually had to start addressing him somehow, and, as you've probably noticed, the poor thing resembles a spider."

"What does he eat? What does he do all day? Does he help you at all?"

Emilia sipped again from her cup.

"I see he really intrigued you. What does he eat? As I said, human fat. I once had a serious problem figuring out what to feed him; now, I don't. I established contact with a few clinics specializing in fat extraction, as a representative of a disposal company. Of course, it required a little deception and magic to make my actions credible, but it worked. And what does he do? I found him an occupation. He knows the kipu[21] system, perhaps he was a priest or official, so I give him important books in Spanish to translate; he reads quite well in that language. He spends his days tying knots."

"For what?"

"I don't really know," admitted the Librarian. "Perhaps it will be useful someday. My goal was more to give him something to do than for the sake of the task itself. It's very tedious, so he has work for decades and feels needed."

"That's a bit sad," Edi whispered.

"Life isn't cheerful. You can't make a paradise out of it. Come, I'll show you the Watchtower." Emilia rose, leaning slightly on her ever-present cane, and headed toward the door.

Edi jumped up eagerly to follow her.

"Excuse me, but why does Aunt limp?" she asked. "Can't it be… well, magically fixed?"

---

[21] Pain, quipu, khipu (in Quechua"knot") - a form of three-dimensional recordused by Indian pre-Columbian South America. Called "knot writing" because of its form: a collection of knots made of cotton or bristleslamy and alpacascolorful strings with knots.

The Grand Librarian looked at the young girl with a slight grimace. Perhaps she wanted to smile, but it didn't come out.

"I fought a battle I couldn't win. Yet I did, though the cost was enormous. In that fight, my *hatzitap*[22]... It's a kind of shorthand, we say that for each of us, because it's always two: Librarian and Grand Librarian. I survived because..." She hesitated. "...I don't actually know why. Something tipped the scales in my favor. I defended the Watchtower, but paid a very high price. What you see now is almost nothing. Had you seen me immediately after the battle, you wouldn't believe I was still alive."

"Who did this to you?"

"Someone behind the Symbiotes, Torque, and many other groups. Someone who thinks he controls Asbiel, though it's rather the other way around. He has one great ambition: to control all available magic. And he pursues it mercilessly."

"So who is he?" The description didn't impress Edi much.

"He goes by the nickname Red Ghost. I had hoped I killed him, but I miscalculated. Asbiel knows how to protect those useful to him, just like—she lowered her voice to a whisper—Woland."

"Which one is stronger?"

---

[22] Hatzi (Hebrew) - half, tapu'ach (henry) – apple.

"Obviously the latter. He is, hmm, evil not only mega-powerful but intelligent and, in his way, elegant. He has principles, can be magnanimous. Asbiel is more primitive, yet extremely ambitious, thus far more dangerous, more aggressive in his actions. Were his powers as great as the Prince of Hell's, I don't even want to think what would happen."

"But they're not?"

"No. Which really annoys that scoundrel. He tries to match him in manipulating humans, but fails. Don't think they're fighting each other. It's far more complicated." She stopped in front of a portrait. "Asbiel cannot act directly, only through humans he has entangled. Like… never mind who. Witches and mages don't want to serve him, so he tries either to coerce them or strip them of their power. Both can only be done using human intermediaries, endowed with supernatural abilities. That's why 'trust no one' is our cardinal rule."

She touched the portrait frame in two places. The large painting slid to the left, revealing spiral stairs leading downward.

CHAPTER VI

The Watchtower... a strange name, Edi thought. More than semantics, she was interested in the place itself. The winding stairs led to an unbelievably vast structure, underground or appearing so. It looked like a museum, mainly consisting of endless tablets, scrolls, and traditional books.

"Oh wow. That's a lot," Edi said, looking around with admiration and curiosity, wondering where to start.

"We have everything, from the very beginnings of knowledge recording."

"And magical textbooks? Do they even exist? Aunt Janina only has one book, and when I asked, she said nobody learns magic from books."

Emilia Gocsary smiled.

"You misunderstood her—or maybe asked the wrong question. You can't learn magic just from the written word. But something like textbooks does exist. Records of mages from all eras, chronicles of their deeds, and so on. You can learn from them primarily what not to do, but also there are thick volumes covering magical plants, simple recipes, monographs on various creatures. Compendia of magical knowledge. If one of 'ours' needs such a book, they borrow it from me; that's why I'm called the Librarian, though 'Keeper of the Collection' would be more accurate."

"Does someone have to come here personally?"

"No, not at all. They just need to ask. There are many ways to send material objects wherever you want, but one must have sufficiently high qualifications."

"And if a book falls into the wrong hands?"

Emilia shrugged.

"Nothing," she said. "To read it, you need the Gift—and more than that. Many have it, but few use it. Some don't even know they have it."

"If it's like Aunt said, someone with the Gift could read the book without knowing they're a potential mage. Then what?"

The Grand Librarian walked slowly among the shelves, stopping before one.

"Nothing," she said. "To read our books, you need not just the Gift, but self-discipline and basic education. You can't imagine what would happen if ordinary people got to our writings. They had to be properly secured, and we did that."

"Reliable?" Edi asked. Emilia smiled again, this time sadly.

"No protection is 100% secure, and humans have always been curious. We have our ways. Have you heard of the Voynich Manuscript?"

The girl frowned.

"Something like that rings a bell," she muttered, discreetly reaching for her smartphone. Emilia Gocsary patiently waited until her young cousin used the browser. Then she took a leather-bound volume from the shelf among countless tomes.

"Oh, Aunt has a copy?" Edi found the page on Google and was reading it.

"The museum has a copy," Emilia snorted. "Damaged, too."

"Wikipedia says no one has been able to decipher it yet."

"They haven't because the museum copy is incomplete and the pages are out of order. If it were different, and someone with the Gift—even an unaware one—examined it…" The older lady opened the book and passed her open hand over it. "…people would learn extremely interesting things. Of course, we ensure there are no leaks, but sometimes something slips. Just like with the Voynich Manuscript. Look now."

The previously undecipherable writing on parchment suddenly softened, becoming ordinary letters forming comprehensible words. Edi's mouth dropped in astonishment.

"Does it work like that on all copies?" she asked.

"Yes, if they're complete. In this way, every mage with literary inclinations records their thoughts and recipes. Not everyone does it, but many. Such private books are priceless; they show the path mages and witches take to their discoveries. And it's necessary. Old spells wouldn't work today; they must be constantly refined, taking changing conditions into account. As I said, magic is a science."

Edi followed Emilia, looking around the shelves with curiosity. She had never seen so many books at once, so varied. Here and there, glass cabinets contained carefully described artifacts, undoubtedly related to the room's theme. They must have been organized according to some system, which she did not yet understand and which interested her less than the exhibits themselves. Something, however, caught her attention.

"Aunt, on that shelf… that's 'Harry Potter,'" she pointed. "And next to it, 'The Witcher'!"

"Yes. We're in the fantasy section," confirmed the Grand Librarian. "We have all books where authors describe something magical. It's my duty to know each and evaluate how dangerous they are. Sometimes a piece of an incantation or ritual description slips in; authors often gain fragments of magical knowledge and reveal them to readers. Then we must immediately deactivate or alter them. It cannot be that an untrained reader, reciting words, triggers, for example, a magic portal. You might think, if they lack magical power, they can chant all they want. True. But you don't know how many people have the Gift, yet, due to character, are unfit for training. Someone like that might accidentally hit the correct intonation or the 'magical moment,' and disaster follows. That's why my work is so important. We cannot remove content from books printed in hundreds of thousands and translated into dozens of languages, but we can neutralize what's contained within. My duty and that of my hatzitap is to read and watch films, identifying potentially dangerous content."

"'The Witcher' has any?"

Emilia snorted dismissively.

"Marginally," she replied. "The author has a knack for linking legendary threads, that's all. But the depiction of a witch fraternity and their activity is complete nonsense. And he unnecessarily injected human ideological issues."

"He had witches helping women, um, terminate unwanted pregnancies," Edi recalled. "I asked Aunt Janina about it once, but she just told me not to bother her."

The Grand Librarian looked embarrassed by the topic.

"I'll teach you about those matters later," she said seriously. "One thing you must know now: we must never come between a person and their destiny. Never. Consequences can be tragic, not just for them."

"So witches didn't do that?"

"Not like us. Magic is not a toy and not for selfish purposes. That doesn't mean... no one does it. But that's a lesson for another time."

They moved to another room, this one without any books. In the center was a television connected to a computer, and shelves held modern media: vinyl records, film reels, cassettes, floppy disks, CDs, DVDs, and USB drives. Each item was carefully labeled. The modern section was modest in size compared to the whole, but still impressively large.

"Does Aunt have movie screenings here? Cool!" Edi began browsing the titles on the discs. Most were familiar, but some she hadn't even heard of.

"I think differently," said Emilia. "Librarians—or Keepers of Knowledge, which is more accurate—must do this, for the reasons I mentioned earlier."

The young girl paused her inspection.

"So even someone who doesn't believe in magic could accidentally cast something?" she asked, seeking confirmation.

She thought this might explain many strange phenomena that have puzzled scientists, but wanted certainty.

Her aunt sighed into one of the club chairs in front of the projector. She massaged her knee, which must have hurt from showing the Watchtower to her cousin.

"One doesn't always use their Gift consciously," she finally said emphatically. "Some even believe it's possible to do so."

Edi shook her head in disbelief.

"So what kind of witches don't actually cast spells?"

"Cocoons. That's what we call them. And they aren't always women. Power affects both sexes equally—it doesn't discriminate." Emilia tapped her cane lightly on the floor. "In cocoons, it manifests in different ways. On the surface, no one would say they aren't ordinary people. They come from different countries, races, social classes, though there is one common trait: exceptional abilities combined with a desperate desire to give as much of themselves to people as they can. And it usually ends badly."

"Why?"

"That's just how it is, my little one. Every mage and witch must pay their dues, even those unaware of their abilities. Especially them. If a cocoon learns to use the Gift, they become a 'spellcrafter' and can channel the fire consuming them from within. Otherwise, it slowly burns them, and worse, attracts all misfortune, like iron filings to a magnet. No one has yet discovered why, but it's a fact."

She rose from the armchair, leaning on her cane, and approached a stand filled with old videotapes. Selecting one, she slid it into the VCR set on the glass table. The television screen lit up, flickered, and a not very clear black-and-white image appeared. A small, unattractive woman with short curls, dressed in a plain black gown almost reaching her ankles, without a single adornment, stood on an empty, bare stage. Only a microphone on a stand and the spotlight surrounded her. From the speaker came the accordion melody, and the static image came to life.

Edi watched, involuntarily frozen in place. The singer remained almost motionless, only her mouth opened in song and hands moving with the rhythm of the melody. A bitter, powerful voice, full of pain, longing, and an immense hunger for love, filled the space, piercing her ears straight to her heart, and Edi felt, to her astonishment, tears sting her eyes.

"Who is she?" she finally managed to ask.

"Edith Piaf," Emilia Gotsary said solemnly. "You are named after her. She needed no playback, no elaborate orchestra, no quadraphonic speakers, special effects, or writhing half-naked on stage in lascivious poses. Bare boards, one spotlight, the cheapest microphone, and someone with an accordion behind her were enough. The entire hall was hers. More than that, the whole world fell to its knees before her. And while she lived, almost no one knew that in the glare of the lights, it would be hard to find a more unhappy, lost person than her. She died prematurely, in great suffering. We didn't know she was one of us—or rather… we found out too late."

Edi looked at the screen again. She couldn't believe it could be true. Since learning about witches, and that she herself was one, she had believed in her own uniqueness. A very pleasant belief. After all, her aunt had long sought the "seventh" for the circle and, despite all efforts, couldn't find anyone. And now it seemed that the Gift wasn't so rare after all.

"Too late? What do you mean?" she asked. "You have that… certain sense, don't you? If she was famous, and you could see her, how didn't you realize?"

Emilia slightly twisted her perfectly shaped lips.

"It's not easy to track a cocoon. Even harder to recognize their potential. Unfortunately, intervention is often too late. Cocoons may gain worldwide fame, lasting fame, but either it brings them no good, or it comes only after their death. Cocoons included Hypatia, Katarzyna Kobro, Masza Iwaszhinova, Frida Kahlo, Zofia Stryjeńska—you probably haven't heard of them. Also Billie Holiday, Camille Claudel, Dalida, Halina Poświatowska. Men: Modigliani, H.P. Lovecraft, Nikola Tesla, Van Gogh, Cyprian Kamil Norwid, Robert E. Howard… Also Vladimir Vysotsky. I suspect Ernest Hemingway too, but not certain. Janis Joplin and Elvis Presley, definitely not. And many others as well, though there were suspicions and we investigated. How many we never detected? We'll probably never know."

Edi furrowed her brow. Something still troubled her.

"Aunt, can the Gift be passed on? Or taken away?" she asked. She remembered a Polish novel she had recently read, "Morrigan," about a witch whose young, inexperienced magical helper mistakenly took her power, turning her into an old, powerless woman.

Emilia sighed lightly.

"The Gift isn't what people generally think it is," she said firmly. "It's a convenient shorthand. There is a Primordial Force that flows through everything in the world. Through some it flows without effect, through others it awakens hidden talents. Being a 'spellcrafter' means realizing this and accepting it without hysteria. You cannot give it or take it away. You simply have it, like hemoglobin in your blood. Do you think it can somehow be gotten rid of?"

"But... if that were so, anyone could use magic!" Edi's disappointment was clear in her voice. She had always thought herself chosen, with exceptional abilities, and now...

Aunt Emilia smiled with subtle superiority, clearly expecting this reaction.

"Well... that's how it is. You just misunderstand. Anyone can use a brush. Art is simple: you just need to know which end to dip in paint. But does that mean anyone can become a world-class painter?"

The young Gwerska shook her head and finally sat down. She suddenly felt tired and overwhelmed. Dom-Na-Skałkach and the Watchtower were very different from Jodełka, whose friendly atmosphere she had grown used to. Now she noticed that darkness prevailed here, unrelated to the level of lighting. A wave of discouragement made her lose the will to speak or ask questions.

The Grand Librarian offered her an elegant cup of white liquid. Edi tasted it automatically and was surprised.

"Milk?"

"Not ordinary, of course. This is Freya's milk. It will make you feel better."

She drank; she was very thirsty. How long had she been here? She looked at her watch and exclaimed.

"Oh my! How late!"

Emilia took the empty cup.

"An illusion."

"What illusion? Half past six in the evening!"

"In the Watchtower and in my house, every personal watch shows relative time. Let's go outside; you'll understand soon."

Outside, the sun shone brightly. Judging its position, Edi did a quick calculation and was astonished.

"It's barely eleven…"

"Exactly eleven-oh-six," Emilia clarified. "I know you worried about reconciling your lessons here with your work with Janka and possible studies. Rest assured, there won't be a problem."

"Librarians manipulate time?!"

The older lady smiled.

"Our abilities are much greater than you think. You'll see soon. But…"

She stopped. From the road beyond a far bend, a young man approached the invisible PKS bus stop. He looked entirely ordinary: fairly tall, a slight overweight, but rather fit. As he got closer, Edi saw a pleasant, boyish face, large glasses, and a cheerful smile.

"Hello, Emilia," he said casually.

"Hello," the Grand Librarian nodded, then turned to her companion. "This is my current hatzitap, Karol Nieściur, present Librarian. Actually, the title is a bit much; he should rather be called a candidate, as he still has much work ahead, though the current situation required his official oath. For now, I authorize decisions on both fronts, and he mainly learns, but to everyone else, he's the new Great Librarian. He's barely older than you, so you'll probably get along well. Karol, this is Edyta Gwerska, my cousin and from today, your student."

"High five, kiddo!" the boy extended his hand warmly. "Are you training to be a Librarian?"

"Not exactly," Edi shook his hand. "I mean… I don't know yet. Maybe. For now, Aunt will give me general training."

"You've got to start somewhere. We'll be buddies, right? Call me Charlie."

"Why that?"

"That's what everyone calls me. Sounds better than Lolek, right? See ya, gotta run."

He entered the house, slightly touching the door with the item in his hand. He was clearly familiar with the place. Edi looked back.

"Aunt isn't coming?"

"Not for now. Karol is mostly self-taught, like every Librarian. Our education is mainly reading—books written by mages and witches. Plus exercises in self-discipline, practicing spells and memory-enhancing potions—quite complex."

"Can you really do that?" Edi asked. "Learn on your own, without a teacher?"

"Yes and no. Such education is an art, requiring real talent. A Librarian must master it, but even then, before becoming a full Guardian, they are under a mentor's guidance, gently pointing them to the right path and providing appropriate materials. But it must be done subtly, especially with individualists like Karol. He can't stand someone above him, so this system suits him. He's also very sensitive—if someone steps on his toes, he charges in regardless of consequences. Better he has no one to clash with. That's mainly why I moved the Watchtower to Poland. He's too young to be separated from his family and homeland, from which he draws strength."

The girl remembered Janina mentioning the same—that witches and mages draw strength from their homeland. Yet something didn't add up.

"If Librarians or Guardians travel the world, and my family did too, how does that fit with the rule?"

Emilia nodded with visible satisfaction.

"You're not stupid. The rule stops applying after a certain development threshold—usually twenty-five to fifty years. After that, the difference between abilities in one's homeland and abroad decreases exponentially. Yet, a spellcrafter is always strongest in their own country. Sometimes it's worth sacrificing a few percent of effectiveness for peace and safety." She patted her cousin on the shoulder. "Go on, child. Come back at the same time tomorrow; we'll start proper training."

CHAPTER VII

Three months can be a long time, or they can be very little.

For someone who went away on a great Greek holiday, they are certainly little; for someone who stayed behind and waited, unbearably long. When Edi finally saw Marek again after more than twelve weeks, she was startled by the changes in him. The boy she had known so well was beginning to resemble a human being less and less. His once ethereal beauty had grown alien and cold, almost repellent. People—especially those who interacted with him every day—might not have noticed how profoundly he had changed, but to the young witch it was obvious at a glance.

"Are you feeling all right?" she asked, returning his friendly kiss of greeting.

He shrugged.

"So-so. I'm having more and more trouble with… with adapting to different situations. And with controlling my power. Finn managed to teach me a thing or two, but since he fell into a coma I've had to cope on my own, and that can be really damn hard. Never mind. How about you?"

They sat down on a low roadside wall.

"I spent the whole morning and most of the late morning helping my aunt during her visits. Do I smell very bad?" Edi asked, looking at him uncertainly.

He sniffed experimentally.

"Moderately," he replied. "Was it rough?"

"I helped vaccinate piglets. An old sow shoved me into a pile of manure and bit my calf. Good thing my aunt was there—it could have been worse. I'll have to be more careful in the future."

"You're not easily discouraged, you little former witch."

She sighed.

"You know what I found out? That I never lost my Gift at all. So not 'former'."

"Well then, congratulations! That's great news. Aren't you happy?" Marek studied her closely. "You don't look exactly thrilled. What is it you actually want?"

Edi shrugged.

"I don't know anymore," she admitted. "What's worse, I have the feeling it doesn't matter whether I want something or not. Life can be insanely complicated."

"You're telling me?" Marek nudged her lightly in the side. "All right, talk. What's got you all tangled up?"

Edi pulled a packet of snack bars from her pocket and handed him one.

"Sugar-free," she said. "Eat without fear. You see, a new aunt has appeared. Well, technically a distant relative, but I call her 'aunt' for simplicity. She's an extremely powerful magician, though she rarely uses her power or knowledge. Mostly she deals with theory. She decided she's going to teach me—though no one bloody asked her to, least of all me."

"That doesn't sound like it makes you very happy," Marek said, unwrapping the bar and taking a bite. "You don't like her?"

"It's not that. She annoys me a little... actually, to the max. I always thought Aunt Janina was old-fashioned, but compared to Emilia she's the very peak of coolness and laid-back charm, if you know what I mean."

"That bad? Maybe it's worth suffering through it a bit if she's teaching you something useful."

"She's a hopeless stiff, like a governess dragged straight out of the nineteenth century," Edi burst out. "Every lesson I feel like if I do or say anything inappropriate I'll get my hands rapped with a switch. What's more, I'm sure she'd actually be ready to do it!"

"You're kidding."

"Well, no—meaning not that she really would," she corrected herself. "I mean that she considers something like that normal. Truly. At first I thought I might manage to like her, but somehow it didn't work. She irritates the hell out of me, and that's that."

"But she teaches you interesting things, right?" Marek took another bite. "It's probably worth the trouble."

"Yeah…" Edi's thoughts drifted back to the previous day.

Emilia Gocsary had been showing her various musical instruments, from the simplest to extremely complex ones.

"Never underestimate the power of melody," she said. "Whenever you hear it, take a moment to consider what it might mean. It is almost the only magical tool that can be successfully used by ordinary people."

"How so?" Edi asked. She wasn't entirely surprised; she had always believed there was something magical about music—especially when it came to one particular composer.

"You've surely heard of excesses at concerts; they can be quite serious. You probably think this is a feature of fans of modern heavy-metal bands or the like, or at most of fans of the Beatles or Elvis Presley—but you'd be wrong. The same thing happened at performances of Paganini or Mozart. Bolesław Prus even described a kind of musical intoxication in *The Doll*. This mechanism was already known to prehistoric people; one day you'll learn from whom they drew that knowledge—during a different lesson, devoted to history."

The librarian picked up the most inconspicuous of the exhibits: two small sticks made of hand-worked wood.

"Do you know what these are?"

"Drumsticks?"

"Almost. They are indeed used for striking, though not a drum, but this." She pointed to a polished human skull. "Do you know the song *Iko Iko*?"

Edi thought for a moment. Something rang a bell, but she couldn't quite place it. Watching her, Emilia hummed, *My granma and your granma…*

"…are sitting by the fire!" Edi exclaimed happily. "Yes, I know it! At first I thought it was about the IKO banking app on a smartphone. I installed it when Aunt Janina started paying me as an assistant."

The older woman nodded.

"Exactly. Almost everyone knows this song; it's very popular. And practically no one realizes how dangerous it is. Its original name was *Chock a Mo*, and it was a Native American war song, usually sung in the Chickasaw language of Louisiana. The words are not particularly important—not even the melody itself—but the properly beaten rhythm, which put warriors into a trance and made them insensitive to pain, even resistant to wounds. Everything depended on the shaman's skill. However, this kind of magic is not strictly martial. It is also used for healing."

She showed Edi two more exhibits: small spherical rattles made of dried gourds.

"Though these little things are usually used for that, not sticks. Both can also successfully replace a tambourine... or a modern drum kit. And in special cases even a rhythm tapped with fingers on anything at all. And I stress—it can be done accidentally."

Edi examined the exhibits with interest. They could have been museum pieces in an ethnographic collection. She shook one of the rattles experimentally; the dry seeds—or perhaps pebbles—inside rustled.

"I once saw a film where a shaman healed someone by rattling over them," she said. "It amused me then. Superstition for simpletons. That's what I thought."

"That is exactly what ordinary people think," Emilia replied. "And they do not associate shamans with the rhythms of popular melodies. That is for the best."

"Can't this be… you know… deactivated somehow? Like the content in films and books you work on?"

Emilia shook her head sadly.

"It is too old a magic. We have no power over it. No one does. It can be used, but it cannot be controlled. No one knows how."

"Not even Woland?"

The older woman shuddered slightly.

"Do not speak his name so loudly or so carelessly," she warned. "I fear he would not let it go so easily and would harass you. That is precisely why you must study as diligently as possible. The stronger you become, the greater your chance of resisting him."

"I'm not afraid of him at all," Edi said, shrugging with an air of superiority.

Her aunt gave her a long, sad look.

"And you should be, my child. All the gods are my witnesses—you should be."

"Were you asleep?" Marek nudged her with his elbow. "This thing really is tasty. Where did you get it?"

"At the Rossmann on Wawelska Street. It's new—I didn't even know such things existed until Ada brought me one once. Lately she's been persuading everyone to give up sugar because it's the white death," Edi blinked drowsily and laughed with a hint of nervousness. "She's gone mad about healthy eating—she studies dietetics at university and it's gone to her head. And you—did you stick with physics?"

He nodded.

"I don't know how to explain it, but this kind of study gives me some kind of anchor, something I can hold on to. I need that to stay among people—and I want to. No matter what."

Edi squeezed his arm.

"I'll help you," she promised. "All of us will. You have friends here. By the way—I just remembered—"

"Yes. Jańcio told me. Is it some sudden illness?"

"Something like that," she replied cautiously, not wanting to say everything yet. "He completely lost his memory. I visit him sometimes, but he still has no idea who I am. We're becoming friends all over again."

"I'll go see him tonight. Maybe he'll recognize me."

"Jańcio already tried, and Ada too," Edi sighed deeply. "Maybe you'll have better luck."

"Shall we go together?"

"Why not?"

For a moment they were silent, watching the cars speeding along the road.

"I found a letter from my uncle in my father's room," Marek said suddenly. "He's here again."

The uncle?! I thought we were rid of him!"

"Yes, him. I mean, he isn't really family at all. And his name isn't Mokrzycki. Mum admitted it when I pressed her. He's some old acquaintance of my father's, has enormous influence over him. Mum probably doesn't know why—or doesn't want to tell me."

Edi frowned.

"What's his real name?" she asked. "Maybe my aunt can find something on him."

Marek hesitated.

"Something dog-like. Rolf... something. The surname was so strange I didn't remember it."

Edi sprang up from the wall.

128

"Come on," she said, holding out her hand. "I'll take you to my aunt. She'll be delighted to meet a real elf, and you can tell her about that bastard."

"She won't be angry?"

"Oh, I don't think so." Just in case, she reached for her smartphone. Although in recent months she had developed the conviction that the Great Librarian knew everything about every step her students took, she decided it would be better to warn her. She dialed a restricted number and put it on speaker.

"Yes, bring him," Emilia's voice said from the phone before Edi could speak. "But not into the house—into the garden behind it. I'll be waiting there."

The screen went dark.

"Wow, she's better than Pegasus!" Marek snorted, amused and impressed. "Your doctor doesn't pull stunts like that, does she?"

Edi shook her head.

"I don't think she can. Nor can my mother. It's some higher-order magic. Come on, we have to catch the bus—we'll ride part of the way; it's not close."

CHAPTER VIII

The area around Crystal Lake lay deserted as far as the eye could see, which was nothing unusual. The body of water, overgrown with reeds and in truth more of a vast pond than an actual lake, occasionally attracted tourists, though only fleetingly. It was not considered an interesting destination for walkers, even if an artist might have found the view picturesque. Among the locals, the place had—so to speak—a bad reputation, and since the inhabitants of the villages around Kraków were particularly fond of superstitions, they avoided it.

The desolate spot was frequented by wandering drunks, looking for a quiet corner to drink cheap wine and—on warmer days—even sleep it off in the grass. The fact that not all of them returned neither surprised nor moved anyone; not even the police took an interest.

"That's just the fate of people from the margins," Fred had once commented. Together with the nymph Alinka, he had more than once driven such a "sleeper" back to the city on a scooter, trying to protect them from rusalkas or drowned spirits

130

roaming the area at night. For obvious reasons, however, they could not help everyone, despite their best intentions. Herta or her companions were sometimes simply faster, and occasionally something more dangerous than they appeared—though rusalkas and dziwożons were more than enough to make a human vanish without a trace. At times it was also the work of rokitkas, who delighted in leading drunkards astray.

Edi was not afraid of Herta or creatures like her. She had no reason to be. While such beings were not friendly toward witches, they respected them. They knew that in a dire situation any witch would help them, and that carried weight. Even so, Janina Batory forbade her niece from going alone to the cursed lake, and Edi's closeness with Herta—objectively useful as it was—greatly displeased the doctor.

"You'll come to no good in the end," she would warn, but the girl paid little attention. She believed she knew best what was good for her, in which she differed little from other teenagers.

Crouching by the water, she lightly splashed it with her finger, which amounted to knocking on a door. After waiting a moment, she repeated the gesture, and almost immediately Herta's golden-haired head emerged from the murky depths, adorned with a water-lily flower.

"Hello, my friend," Edi said warmly.

Herta swam closer and rested her elbows on the bank.

"Hello, little witch," she replied. "How are things? All right?"

"Well… not really. Aunt Emilia is inviting you to the House-on-the-Rocks. She wants to—talk."

The rusalka opened her beautiful, pale green eyes wide and pondered.

"Emilia Gocsary?" she asked to be sure. "If that's so, then things must be bad. Very bad."

She hauled herself onto dry land, her wet dress clinging to her body and covered in duckweed. Straightening up, she brushed the fabric with her hands. It dried instantly, and the little leaves fell to the ground with a soft rustle. The rusalka's lovely hair lifted and twisted itself into a neat bun, and fashionable shoes appeared on her narrow feet.

"Well then, let's go."

Edi had seen such transformations before—simple as breathing for rusalkas. She envied them a little for that ability, which allowed them, effortlessly and for a short time, to blend into human society whenever they wished. And that was far from all they could do. They did not need to learn magic; it was instinctive, innate, and wonderfully easy for them.

The aspiring witch had hoped to be present during her aunt's conversation with Herta, but she was disappointed.

Emilia curtly told her to "mind herself," which meant she had no time for her. That sometimes happened when the Great Librarian was working on an urgent matter. In such cases, her student had permission to roam freely through the Watchtower and examine whatever she pleased, on the condition that she took notes about what she saw and what intrigued her. Later, she discussed them with her aunt.

The sheer scale of the place and its contents ensured that boredom was impossible. The artifacts displayed in glass cases were fitted with miniature seals so they posed no danger, allowing her to handle them without risk. Most were entirely unfamiliar to her. She did not know what they were, what they meant, or what they might be used for. Some looked like crude handicrafts made of wood, clay, or stone; others were true masterpieces of jewelry, which she admired with genuine pleasure and occasionally even tried on in front of a mirror. And mirrors were everywhere in the Watchtower, hanging on every scrap of free wall space. Edi suspected they were magical, though for now she had no proof.

This time, however, the offended Gwerska protested.

"If Marek is staying, why not me?"

"Because no," Emilia replied sternly. "We'll talk about it later. Go explore, look at whatever you like. Karol is in the Watchtower—if you have questions, ask him. Araña is in his room, but if you happen to run into him, don't be afraid. He knows who you are. He won't hurt you."

"I'm not afraid of him."

"Perhaps you should be. The level of today's youth is terrifying—you have no imagination whatsoever. Now go."

Edi looked at Marek for support, but he merely shrugged. He himself had no idea why his presence was necessary for the conversation and hers unwelcome. Realizing she would gain nothing, she snorted, spun on her heel, and headed toward the house. Angry at the whole world, she showed the door open and slammed it shut behind her.

"Dirty trick," she muttered under her breath.

She didn't feel like going down to the Watchtower just yet. Instead, she decided to finally explore Emilia's private residence properly. Until now there had never really been an opportunity—she had only seen the living room and kitchen, and the living quarters extended much farther. Here, however, another disappointment awaited her. The rooms looked perfectly ordinary. Only the second sitting room, at the end of the corridor, seemed interesting. Dark walnut furniture that probably dated back to the eighteenth century stood there; a fire burned in the fireplace, and beside it stood a small table with a magnificent crystal sphere. As Edi judged, it could not have been made of ordinary glass—the reflections of the flames scattered into multicolored sparks within it, like those of a huge diamond. She admired it without touching, just in case.

At last she decided to peek into the room where—she knew—Araña resided.

CHAPTER IX

The meeting convened by Emilia Gocsary did not end until late in the evening, and only then did the Watchtower open, releasing both students. They both had the impression that nearly a full day had passed, though in reality it had been only a few hours. They had hoped to learn more, but the Great Librarian showed no eagerness to explain her actions.

"You don't need to know everything," she replied to the barrage of questions. "In fact, you shouldn't. Your task is to learn. Serious matters will be handled by those who have either completed their education—or have no need of one. Off you go. Now."

Without listening to what the young people still had to say, she went into the house and shut herself in her bedroom. She looked utterly exhausted and, worse still, discouraged.

"Go," Karol nudged Edi in the side. "I'll stay here. I'll wait until she gets some sleep—maybe she'll be more talkative then. I'll call you later. Hey, who's that guy?" He pointed at a slim blond man leaning against the wall. "I don't know him. He was in the garden."

"That's my guy," the girl waved to catch his attention. "I'm here!"

The young man pushed himself away from the wall and walked over.

"Hi. Marek Mokrzycki." He held out his hand to Karol, who introduced himself automatically. "Edi's my friend."

"Mine too," the student of magic shook his hand warmly. "Great girl, right? And you…" He squinted at him. "You're an elf! Holy crap!"

Marek looked at Edi questioningly.

"Charlie's training in recognizing non-humans," she explained. "He's an adept of the magical sciences."

"Nice to meet you. I'm an adept of solid-state physics. Ask Mrs. Emilia about the rest," he added lightly. "We'll talk later. Shall we go? It's really late. I'll visit Szkrab tomorrow."

"Sure. Pick me up and we'll go together."

"The one who lost his memory?" Karol, already heading back to the house, glanced over his shoulder. "I'll send you something by text in a minute. It should help."

He quickened his pace and disappeared behind the door.

"Adept?" Marek sounded doubtful. "Why not just a mage? A regular human wouldn't have recognized me."

She shrugged.

"I don't know. He definitely knows some things, but he's more about gathering knowledge than using it in practice. Like Aunt Gocsary. I think that's what the Guardians are for. I think he likes me," she giggled. "Just a little."

"Let's head for the bus stop and catch the bus. They're probably wondering back at Jodełka whether I've been kidnapped," Edi glanced at her watch.

"Oh, come on. You're an adult, aren't you?"

"Not really, as far as they're concerned."

She didn't add that it bothered her less now than it once had—more than that, she was starting to appreciate it. She had a loving, if slightly odd, family she could rely on. That was priceless, even if they were sometimes overprotective of the 'baby' of the family.

"What was your aunt talking to all of you about?" she asked as they walked toward the bus stop.

Her friend glanced at her sideways.

"You won't rat me out?"

"Come on."

"She basically announced something like a general mobilization. I didn't understand everything, but apparently nymphs, rusalkas, drowned spirits, forest devils and all those 'types' don't usually live in harmony. They coexist separately, each convinced they're better than the others. Once a year they get together for a joint celebration—that's tradition. But now a common enemy has appeared. From now on it's 'one for all, all for one.' And why? That Olf who pretended to be my uncle has some kind of plan."

"Definitely. But what kind?" Edi watched him closely.

"Aunt Gocsary says he wants to take control of the... magical field? I'm not sure what to call it. She used a lot of strange terms. I lost the thread at times. I understood it like this: magic is like a massive internet portal that witches, mages and all sorts of creatures can access at different levels—full access, limited access, conditional access, user access, admin access, moderator access. And Olf wants control. He wants to change all the passwords so only he can use the portal."

"Then he'd dictate the rules."

"Exactly."

"Did she say whether that's even possible? Technically, I mean."

"Very difficult—but possible. He has the backing of a powerful demon. That's why cooperation on an unprecedented scale is necessary. Everyone has to be involved."

"He might think of that too."

"It won't help him, even if he does." Marek stopped walking. "Edi, I never believed in abstract good and evil. I thought they were just simplified concepts. But they're not. Evil exists—and it's very strong. Stronger than good."

She shuddered.

"Does that mean—?"

"No," he cut her off. "Remember *The Pilot Pirx Test*? Weakness can be a weapon if you know how to use it. And strength can be a weakness. From what I understood your aunt to say, the strength of good lies in equal cooperation. Evil doesn't cooperate with anyone—not even with itself."

"I've read that somewhere too," she frowned, trying to remember where.

"Doesn't matter. Evil only knows how to dominate—or be dominated by something stronger. Olf wants everything for himself. He doesn't want to share, not even with Asbiel, whose subcontractor he is. His ambition is to bind the demon, who probably knows this and finds it amusing—for now. Another weakness of evil: it cannot appreciate anyone it considers weaker. That always comes back to bite."

They walked in silence for a while.

"So… war?" Edi finally asked, trying to sound indifferent.

"Looks like it. You and I will be part of it too. We don't have much choice—it's a high-level game, and we're cannon fodder."

"Only if we allow it. Learn to use your talents. Finn is still in a coma, but ask Aunt Emilia to find you another mentor. I'll put in the effort too. It's not true that nothing depends on us. If we want it to—and work for it—it will."

Marek smiled, and his still half-human face transformed into the perfect features of an elf.

"You're growing up right before my eyes, girl."

When they reached Jodełka, it was already past midnight. The light was on in the living room, and through the window they could see the silhouette of a woman sitting in an armchair with a book. From the outline of her hairstyle it was clear that it was Jadwiga Gwerska.

"They're waiting for me," Edi said quietly, stopping.

"Want me to go in with you?"

"No, they won't bite my head off. I'll see you tomorrow. Around eleven? Or better yet, be at the bus stop."

"Sure." Marek kissed her on the cheek. "Good luck."

He walked away, melting into the darkness. The girl lingered for a moment, savoring the night sounds and the smell of nature. Depending on the wind, the scent of forest, grass and flowers was generously enriched by the stench of manure or barns—but one could get used to that. Contrary to idyllic descriptions, the countryside doesn't smell of violets, which often painfully surprises city dwellers seeking 'contact with nature.' They are shocked to discover that nature is simply brutal, primitive, and utterly unpoetic—that cute farm animals are dirty, produce tons of foul-smelling waste, and can maim or even kill; that fashionable shoes sink into mud, dogs bark, and roosters wake people at night and at dawn. On top of that, farm machinery cannot work quietly and doesn't respect Sundays or holidays during the season. Big-city residents who move to rural areas often take this as a personal affront and sometimes even report it to the police.

Edi smiled to herself. Though she had grown up in the city, she had never had trouble with rural conditions and found people amusing who wanted to live in agricultural areas without the slightest understanding of reality. Then she remembered someone waiting for her inside and hurried almost at a run to the door.

The moment she entered the living room, she put on a contrite expression—just in case.

"I'm sorry, Mom," she chirped. "The Watchtower—"

"I know," Jadwiga interrupted. "Emilia sent us a message. Besides, you're of age." She sighed deeply. "I truly don't want to be the kind of mother who expects her child to cling to her skirts forever. Still, don't be surprised if in situations like this... I wait for you until you come back."

Touched, Edi stepped forward and hugged her tightly.

"I know, Mom. And I appreciate it. Truly."

"Let's say," Jadwiga patted her back. "We didn't have a normal relationship when you were a child. It's hard to make up for that now, but I want you to know that you have always— always—been the most important thing in the world to me."

The young girl sat down on the footstool beside the armchair and rested her head on her mother's knees.

"I know, Mom. I understand many things now that I didn't before. Is Aunt Janina asleep?"

"She's not home. Little Obrędzki called and asked her to come over. Probably another horse with colic."

"Maciek?" Edi raised her head, frowning. "Maciek called? Why not his father?"

"Apparently he's not home, and there were no adults there. The boy was afraid to wait."

"That might make sense…"

Jadwiga smiled uneasily.

"It seems strange to me too, but Janka grabbed her bag and ran off like it was a fire. Maybe precisely because something didn't add up for her either. We'll talk to her tomorrow. Now off to bed—you're falling asleep on your feet. I'll go lie down too."

The next day Janina did not appear at the house until Edi, well rested and fresh from her morning shower, was standing in the kitchen wondering whether to make scrambled eggs or fried eggs for her late breakfast. Without paying any attention to her, the veterinarian poured herself a full mug of coffee from the pot and drained it in one gulp.

"Did the horse recover?" Edi asked, cracking the eggs one by one into a bowl.

Janina lowered the mug from her lips.

"What horse?" she asked dully. She glanced at the table. "You're making scrambled eggs? Throw in three more for me. And add some onion."

"Bacon or butter?"

"Bacon. I'm going to wash up."

Since in the Batory household frying eggs was something of a ritual, Janina managed to shower and change before the

144

deliciously fragrant dish landed on the table in the living room. Sister and niece waited for the doctor to sit down and began eating the moment she did.

"Where's Fred?" Janina asked, heaping a generous portion onto her plate.

"At Oxygen," Jadwiga replied. "He's doing an inventory. Alinka is helping him—or at least that's her intention. Knowing nymphs, that help is rather debatable."

"What's an inventory?" Edi asked with interest.

"A kind of stock-taking in libraries," her mother explained. "Janka, what about that visit to the Obrędzkis? Was it really about a horse? Because I have my doubts. You know I know you, so don't lie."

For a moment the veterinarian ate in silence. Then she raised her head from her plate.

"No. It wasn't about any animal," she admitted. "Obrędzki was shot and needed help."

"Why didn't he call an ambulance?"

"What do you think? A gunshot wound isn't a broken leg. There'd be the police, the prosecutor, an investigation. And that man runs various businesses that are a bit... off, and he knows people he shouldn't. That simply wasn't an option."

Jadwiga put down her spoon and grew serious.

"Sis, what have you gotten yourself into?" she asked sharply. "Why are you mixing yourself up in some kind of mafia business?"

Janina shrugged.

"Mafia, please. Some mafia—maybe for the poor. Obrędzki does like to pose as, how shall I put it, a sort of pocket-sized Al Capone, but that's not my problem. Let the proper services deal with him, and if they can't prove anything, let them hang themselves. They can arrest someone for stealing a candy bar, right? So if a businessman like him has something on his conscience, all the more reason they should be able to nail him. Apparently they've got nothing."

"You sound like some political activist. I don't recognize you!"

The veterinarian poured herself more coffee.

"Don't exaggerate, sister," she said. "I'm not a cop or a lawyer, and Obrędzki's shady dealings are none of my concern—nor anyone else's. I'm a veterinarian. The man takes excellent care of his animals, so when he calls me, I go. And that this time it was his son who called, and in a situation like that— well, so be it. I like that kid. He was terrified and didn't know who to turn to, and he trusts me."

"Auntie, could it be that Obrędzki killed whoever shot at him?" Edi interjected.

Doctor Batory shook her head.

"No. They wanted to eliminate him. I questioned him in my own way and I know that although he has a thing or two on his conscience, he hasn't killed anyone—yet. Some Georgian gang wants to take over his businesses, so blood will probably still be spilled one way or another. Don't look at me like that, Jadźka, you know how it is. People are like this. Neither of us was born yesterday, or even the day before. Gangs existed, exist, and will exist, just like illegal businesses. And it's not our affair. We don't get involved."

"You just did."

With a sigh, Janina took a sip of coffee and finished her now-cold scrambled eggs.

"No. I only helped as a doctor. All right, a veterinarian—but what is a human, if not a mammal?"

"Will he survive?" Edi asked quietly.

"Yes. Though it was very serious. I had to use strong magic. No, Jadźka, I didn't break the Fifth Rule of the Code. It's not that bad yet."

"What Code?" the girl asked. "What rule?"

"You still have time for both," Jadwiga said sternly. "The code of ethics—"

"It's more of a self-preservation code," her sister cut in.

"—is for licensed magic practitioners, not for students," Mrs. Gwerska continued, ignoring her. "You fortunately don't have the capacity to break it. It can't be done by accident. It requires not only talent, but skill. And those aren't acquired over years, but over entire decades of practice."

"All right, but why didn't I even know there was a code at all?" Edi asked.

"And why should you? For now that knowledge wouldn't do you any good."

Janina tapped her plate to draw attention.

"Not entirely, Jadźka. Your little one is quite a handful. Sometimes strange things work out for her just like that— without much effort. Maybe it would be better to make her aware of certain things in advance? Today's youth matures quickly, and people like her"—she gestured with her spoon toward Edi—"are clearly part of that."

Jadwiga looked at her daughter as if seeing her for the first time.

"You must be joking."

"No. She healed a badly injured girl after an accident and got her back on her feet. She did it instinctively, without even knowing how. Emilia probably doesn't know about this particular incident."

"You think so?"

"She never mentioned it, and I think she would have. In any case, Edi is one big statistical impossibility. Who knows what she'll do next. In my opinion, it would be wise to introduce her to the Code now, before she causes trouble for herself and for us."

"As if you were blameless in all this," Jadwiga snapped. "Look who's coming."

She pointed out the window. Janina and Edi turned and saw the familiar silhouette of a police officer approaching Jodełka. The veterinarian sighed.

"Herman... of course. He's a detective. If Obrędzki's name surfaced, I might have crossed his mind—he knows I treat the man's animals. He warned me about him."

"You should have listened."

"Leave me alone. It's my life."

Janina jumped up from her chair, quickly brushed her tousled hair in front of the mirror and drew lipstick across her mouth. She managed to straighten and cinch her house dress with a belt just before the policeman pressed the doorbell.

"Let's go to the garden. No one will bother us there," she suggested, opening the door and pulling Herman Wiszewski along before he could reply.

Jadwiga snorted in disapproval.

"Childish."

"Oh, come on, Mom. You were in love too. You even got married," Edi glanced at her watch and sprang up from the table. "Oh crap, I forgot I'm meeting Marek. He's probably already waiting. Bye, Mom."

On her way to the PKS bus stop she remembered Karol's text message. She pulled her smartphone from her pocket and reread the short message: *"One hand on the nape, the other on the forehead, and act."*

"Easy to say," she muttered. Personally, she didn't feel like someone who could heal. The memorable incident with Tosia had remained in her mind as a case in which she had rather been used as a conduit of power—as if someone else had acted through her. Who had done it, and why, she still didn't know.

"Or maybe not?" she wondered aloud. "Maybe that was just my impression, and it was wrong? After all, what do I really know?"

She quickened her pace. Her watch showed quarter to eleven, and she knew Marek would already be waiting. His punctuality sometimes bordered on obsession—what else could you call showing up a good half hour early to every meeting? Edi didn't like being late either, but she didn't treat it with such deadly seriousness, considering her friend's scrupulousness at least excessive. Well, that was just how he was, and one had to accept it. All the more concerned she became when she reached the stop and didn't see him there.

She looked around helplessly, then checked her watch again. Ten minutes to eleven. Technically still time, but she felt a sharp twinge of unease.

"Marek!" she called out. She had little hope of an answer— apart from the bus shelter, there was nothing within a hundred meters where an elf could hide. Just a few low raspberry bushes growing along the edges of a shallow ditch, too sparse to conceal anyone. Beyond that the forest began; on the other side lay harvested fields. Buildings in the distance. Not a soul in sight.

Confused, the girl looked around once more, unsure what to do. Then she reached for her smartphone, but her friend's phone remained stubbornly silent. That was starting to look suspicious. She stood there for a moment, trying to think, when her attention was caught by a strange, mewling sound. She recognized it somehow. It sounded a bit like a peacock's call, but it definitely wasn't one.

She looked around again and, straining her eyes, finally noticed something lurking beneath one of the bushes. Something small—not a cat, not a dog, but an animal that seemed oddly familiar. Intrigued, she headed toward the ditch. When she got closer, she realized it was a bird, resembling a large dark-yellow hen, or rather a rooster with a comb drooping to the left. The creature looked at Edi plaintively and opened its beak—not long and narrow, but short and broad, like that of birds of prey—emitting those incongruous, mewling sounds. The girl crouched down.

"What are you doing here, Buczek?" she asked, extending her hand. "Do you need help? Or do you want to tell me something? Sorry, I don't have any food."

Of all the little creatures called *ubożęta* in old writings, this one stirred the tenderest feelings in her. She didn't know why. Perhaps it was the voice, perhaps the look in its eyes, or perhaps its apparent helplessness, silently crying, *Take care of me.* Legends said that yielding to that mute plea could end badly, but that wasn't entirely true. Nothing bad ever happened to a person who treated a kłobuk honestly.

Edi stroked the creature's silky feathers. They weren't wet at all; they only looked that way, and to the touch they resembled the delicate down on a pigeon's belly. The kłobuk raised its head and looked her in the eyes. It mewed again, then got up on its little legs and scampered a short distance toward the forest. It stopped and looked back at her.

"Do you want me to follow you?"

It seemed that it did. She went after it. She had to quicken her pace because the creature was almost running, but when they crossed the line of trees, it suddenly stopped and turned its head. The girl stopped too, waiting to see what would happen. It stared stubbornly, not at Edi, but somewhere beyond her.

She turned around and saw that the bus shelter was no longer empty. Three people were there—two men and a woman. Instinctively, Edi crouched behind a blackberry bush, long stripped of fruit by local children. Only then did she realize that—without even knowing she was doing it—she had sharpened her vision, just as she once had her hearing. As if she were looking through binoculars.

No, she didn't know these people, but one of the men, slim and blond, at first seemed to be Marek—so much so that she felt a momentary wave of relief. But it wasn't him. He was only wearing Marek's distinctive hoodie, a branded Reebok with a hood. She remembered it had cost him a lot; he'd saved for a long time to buy it and wore it on cooler days. She was sure it was the same one, not just a similar hoodie. It had a characteristic patch sewn onto the sleeve to hide a red dye stain. He'd splashed it one day when he and his friends were fooling around in the school library, making ink blots on official paper with printer ink. Mrs. Mokrzycka had sewn on the patch because Marek didn't want to throw the hoodie away—he liked it too much, and it had cost too much—and the ink couldn't be removed.

The other man and the woman were dressed almost identically: light brown trousers, denim vests over checked shirts, and high combat boots. Painfully ordinary. If not for the one clearly trying to impersonate Marek, Edi wouldn't have paid them much attention at all. But now…

She focused the way Emilia had taught her, and after a moment her ears began working like a directional radar. She couldn't maintain that state for longer than a minute—it required too much effort—but she hoped that would be enough.

"…girls like that are always late," the woman was saying. She kicked a small stone with the tip of her boot. "Pull the hood down more so she doesn't realize."

"Maybe she won't come?" the one in the jacket shrugged.

"I don't know. She called a few minutes ago. Maybe she wanted to say she'd be late."

"You should've answered."

"Are you stupid? She'd recognize right away that it wasn't his voice. She's a witch, for heaven's sake. Relax—she'll come for sure." The woman scanned the area carefully.

Edi curled up even tighter, trying to be invisible. The kłobuk pressed against her calf. She laid her hand on its back, feeling the silky feathers and friendly warmth beneath her fingers. She was grateful to the strange creature for its silent presence; she felt priceless support from it, without which fear might have overwhelmed her. Because she was afraid. For the first time in a long while, she was truly afraid.

The man in Marek's hoodie pulled an iPhone from his pocket.

"I'll text her," he suggested.

Edi flinched. She could no longer maintain the "zoom" spell and had to let it go, but truth be told, she'd heard enough. Her smartphone vibrated softly. She pulled it from her pocket with trembling fingers and unlocked it.

"Hey, I'm here, waiting," read the message under the name MAREK.

She wasn't sure she was doing the right thing, but she replied, *"On my way."* It might buy her some time—but time for what, exactly? For some action? She couldn't think of anything. She only hoped they wouldn't start searching the area. They could easily conclude that someone might be hiding among the trees, and then… Would she manage to escape? Fighting in this situation probably made no sense; they were surely prepared.

"Buczek, what am I supposed to do?" she whispered helplessly.

Pressed against her leg, the kłobuk lifted its head and mewed almost soundlessly. Unlike many other fantastic creatures, it couldn't speak—or perhaps didn't want to. But it could somehow influence humans, because under the impact of its gaze the girl came up with an idea. She had never used this trick before; she didn't even know if it would work. Karol had taught her the technique, but she'd never had a chance to test it. Urged on by the kłobuk's stare, she pressed the pads of her index fingers to her temples and began to whisper the formula. She desperately hoped she wouldn't make a mistake. The sequence of words and numbers was so nonsensical that she couldn't rely on typical mnemonic tricks. And this particular one the young Librarian had praised as very useful. The time had come to say *Check*—she just couldn't afford to get anything wrong.

For a moment she felt as if nothing was happening. Then someone appeared on the road leading to the bus stop. A stooped old woman in a long black dress and an equally black headscarf. She shuffled along slowly, dragging her feet, as if her back hurt. Edi bit her lower lip. She thought she recognized the figure, but she didn't want to jinx it, so she merely held her breath and watched, trying to sharpen her sight just a little.

The woman in black reached the bus stop and suddenly straightened up. The scarf slipped from her head onto her shoulders, revealing gray hair spilling around a pale, elongated face. She no longer looked like a harmless old woman; an extraordinary, sinister power radiated from her entire figure. She raised her hands, and a huge bouquet of lupins appeared in them. She swept it in front of the stunned people's faces. The sun shining in the clear sky seemed to flare brighter for a moment, and almost immediately all three collapsed to the ground, motionless.

"You can come out now!" the Południca called, looking toward the line of the forest.

Edi abandoned her hiding place and reached the bus stop as fast as she could.

"Thank you!" she panted, grabbing her rescuer's hand. "Did you hear my call?"

"You're welcome. We all heard it. I was the closest. Who are these people?"

"I don't know. They were going to catch me. I'm afraid they hurt my friend." Edi crouched down and, with some effort, pulled Marek's hoodie off the unconscious blond man. "This one was dressed as him. And he has Marek's iPhone in his pocket."

"Take their documents too," the Południca advised. "They must have some. You don't need to be careful—I gave them sunstroke."

"Serious?"

"They'll die from it if no one finds them."

The young witch hesitated.

"Still… that's not right."

"Not for you," the harvest wraith agreed. "But I don't have such limitations. I am part of the force of nature, and it is not sentimental."

"What am I supposed to do now? Please, advise me!" the girl burst out desperately. "I feel that something very bad is happening! I've never been this scared before…"

She fell silent under the cold, indifferent gaze of the Slavic demon, suddenly short of breath at the thought of whom she was speaking to, whom she was asking for help.

"Your time has come," the Południca said after a moment. "From now on, you make your own decisions. Good or bad— but your own."

She turned away and left, dissolving into a thin mist that the wind scattered over the stubble fields.

CHAPTER X

The sanctuary looked the same as always; only the statue of the unidentified deity was crowned with intertwined ears of rye and wheat. The priestess was just decorating them with rowan berries.

"I—I'm sorry," Edi said to her hesitantly. "The kłobuk brought me here. I need to speak with the Mother."

The priestess glanced at her.

"She knows," she said calmly. "She's waiting for you in the temple."

"What temple?"

"There." She pointed to the statue.

For the first time, Edi noticed that it was not a monolith, as she had always assumed. Between the thickened shapes that were probably meant to represent the forgotten god's arms, there was a narrow, slit-like entrance leading inward. She had never seen it before and had never even suspected its existence. Had she been granted another initiation?

Hesitantly, she approached. She glanced again at the priestess, who, no longer paying her any attention, continued weaving rowan branches into the garlands of grain. Realizing she could expect no help from her, Edi stepped into the darkness and stopped. She felt the warm body of the kłobuk against her leg; it had clearly decided not to leave her, and that gave her courage. She took one step forward, then another—and the darkness ended as abruptly as if cut with a knife.

The girl found herself in a circle of gentle light cast by a bluish crystal suspended beneath the grotto's vaulted ceiling. Żywia sat in the center on a stone throne, reached by several worn steps.

"Welcome, my child," the goddess said. "I know why you have come."

"I have no idea what to do," the girl confessed. "Some monster has begun hunting me—and probably not only me."

"Not you at all," Żywia leaned her head back against the high, dragon-carved stone backrest of the throne. "You are an insignificant pawn in his game. At least, that is how he sees it."

"Who is he?"

"Sit," Żywia said, indicating a low footstool on the dais. "I will tell you something. Matthew Hopkins—have you heard of him? The most famous and best-paid Witchfinder in the history of the British Isles. He was called 'the terror of Manningtree.' He operated in the seventeenth century, and his victims were, unfortunately, mostly ordinary village women. He had a genuine gift for recognizing witches, but fortunately for them he did not know how to use it properly. True witches quickly learned how to protect themselves from him; he managed to catch two, perhaps three. The rest of his victims were entirely innocent. Greed was his downfall. He used dishonest methods to prove he was right, and eventually this came to light. Not long afterward he died—supposedly of tuberculosis, though I would not be so sure. Before departing this world, however, he fathered several children. Each inherited the Hunter's gift from him. One of this man's descendants—and the most gifted of them—is Olf Rødtspøgelse. But he inherited not only that unique trait; he also inherited extraordinary ambition and insane greed. And from his mother, an intelligence surpassing that of most people. It is a dangerous combination, my daughter."

"He wants absolute power."

"Yes. He has devised a detailed plan to exterminate all beings such as nymphs, rusalkas, fauns, or even kłobuks like this one," she gestured toward the creature crouched beside Edi. "This, of course, also applies to witches and mages who refuse to serve him. And even those who do serve him should consider themselves at risk."

"Why?" the shocked girl asked, her eyes widening.

"For at least three reasons. First, he believes the world should belong to humans—and only to humans. Second, because he knows they will never submit to him. Never. And he cannot bear that."

"And the third?"

"To prevent them from drawing upon the sources of power and thus diminishing their reserves. For now, of course, he cannot do very much. As you know, he attempted to seize the Watchtower, which would have given him a powerful weapon—knowledge. The Librarians risked everything they had to stop him, and they succeeded, though at a tremendous cost. The Watchtower was further secured—or rather, it secured itself. It can do that, but it does not act preemptively. It responds to new threats only once they actually arise, creating advanced barriers. However, it needs time to do so, and that time is not always granted. That is why Karol had to become the Grand Librarian, even though he is not ready."

Edi pondered what she had heard in silence for a moment. It sounded bad. Very bad.

"Mother… surely someone like you cannot be harmed by him?" she asked at last, hoping her voice would not tremble.

Żywia sighed softly and placed her hand on the girl's head.

"My child, lesser gods cannot act—or even exist—without their worshippers. The greatest ones… well, that is a mystery even I do not know. But think about it: Their—or perhaps His, or Hers, I do not know—once almost daily interference in human affairs suddenly ceased when materialism came into fashion on a mass scale."

"That's why there's such pressure to atheize societies!" young Gwerska exclaimed. "So that the gods lose their power! Someone is fighting the gods!"

"Yes. And not since yesterday. It has been going on for centuries. Once it was little more than a harmless eccentricity of a group of fanatics, but today—"

"Wait," Edi tried to arrange it all into a coherent picture, and something did not add up. "Shouldn't demons draw their power from the same source?"

The goddess shook her head. She looked tired and discouraged.

"Demons draw their strength from what is evil in humans— from their selfish desires and inclinations. And there will always be more than enough of that. Once, at least, people tried to keep up appearances. They were ashamed of evil, of moral filth, even if they succumbed to it. And that weakened demons. Today it is different. What should never be a source of pride is considered one. There has been a complete reversal of the concepts of good and evil—not for the first time in human history—but if you take the trouble to study the subject, you will see how it ended every time."

For several minutes Edi remained silent. Then she looked Żywia straight in the face.

"Can't something be done?" she asked.

"No. Any intervention from above would only make matters worse. The gods know this. All of them—not only those like me, whose power is limited to a single region."

"Then what is the point of my training?"

The question hung in the air, and time seemed to stop. Everything froze for a moment.

"People like you are the last hope," the goddess finally spoke, her voice like the rustling of wind. "You are the ones who still maintain the fragile balance in this mad world. Through you—thanks to you—we can act. You hold back destruction."

"Do demons want to destroy humanity?"

Żywia managed a faint, bitter laugh.

"No, my child. Humans are the sine qua non of their existence. Gods existed before humans and may exist after them—but not demons. They are inextricably bound to humanity, even Woland, though he would never admit it. No, only humans threaten humans. That is why any help is so difficult."

Edi looked at the folded hoodie she still held in her hand.

"Marek… That man abducted Marek! I have to save him."

The goddess's fingers—slender and delicate—tightened warningly on the crown of her head with a strength Edi had not expected.

"No."

"What do you mean, no?"

"You must write off that elf. Do you understand me, child?"

"But I—"

"Listen. All bearers of elven blood are highly susceptible to manipulation in early childhood. They can be programmed like clockwork dolls. Trained like dogs. And that is exactly what happened. Your friend was not abducted. He went with Olf of his own free will, the moment Olf whistled for him."

Edi stared at her in disbelief.

"That's impossible!"

"More is possible than you can imagine, my poor child."

The girl wanted to protest further, but she remembered the Watchtower's reaction—strange, almost excessive. But why had Emilia Gocsáry sensed nothing? She, the Grand Librarian, deceived in such a crucial matter? Żywia sighed again.

"Your aunt could sense nothing," she said, clearly reading the young witch's thoughts. "The boy himself did not realize at the time how deeply conditioned he had been by someone he had regarded almost his entire life as his uncle. Have you heard of a 'reverse exorcism'?"

"No. Only of ordinary exorcisms."

"Few people today believe in their effectiveness anyway."

"To be honest, neither do I," Edi admitted. "It's so… old-ladyish. Smells of medieval superstition."

"And what do you know of the Middle Ages?" Żywia asked. "It was a period of flourishing science, art, and architecture—not a dark age, as it is now portrayed. Yet today one merely says 'the Middle Ages,' and that becomes the ultimate argument—that something is outdated, ridiculous, lacking scientific basis or deeper meaning."

"Well… science *has* advanced a great deal over those centuries," the girl objected.

"Hardly surprising. We can discuss this another time. Right now there are more important matters than a history lesson. Back to the point. A 'reverse exorcism' is a controlled alteration of personality in a person who has a dual one."

"Like split personality?"

Żywia frowned, her beautiful brow creasing. The fingers still resting on the girl's head worked like a transmitter, searching Edi's mind for appropriate words. The proto-Slavic goddess did not possess a vocabulary extensive enough to converse freely with a representative of an internet-educated generation. She needed access to the girl's mind and her lexicon.

"Not exactly," she said at last. "In dissociation, we are dealing with two or more souls in one body. Dual personality concerns a single soul that perceives the world differently. It is not that control of someone—let us say Jan—is taken over by Adam, but that Jan changes from a good man into a bad one, which he might have become anyway if the shaping of his character had taken a different turn."

"Oh wow. That sounds bad," Edi muttered. The fingers tangled in her hair twitched.

"Worse than you think. A pure-blooded elf, acting as Olf's hound, will be dangerous. Beware of him," the goddess grimaced. "It seems it had to be this way. There are things I cannot change. I can only warn you and give you my blessing."

"So Marek, as Sapkowski wrote, was born in the shadow of destiny?" Gwerska recalled a passage from *The Witcher* and could not help herself.

"I know no Sapkowski. Every human is born in the shadow of destiny. Everyone. But people misunderstand what that word means." Żywia finally withdrew her hand, breaking the connection. "This is not a conversation for today. We will return to it at a more appropriate time. Take your kłobuk now and go home."

The girl looked in astonishment at the creature pressed against her calf.

"What do you mean, *my* kłobuk?"

"Yours. It chose you, and now it is yours. Take good care of it, and it will repay you. It is a friendly house spirit, despite what is sometimes said."

Janina Batory, preparing to leave for a house call, froze by the open door of her jeep when she saw her niece with the kłobuk in her arms. She was already opening her mouth to deliver a lecture, but when she caught sight of Edi's drawn face, she abandoned the idea. For the first time, she had the impression she was looking at a grown woman. She even blinked. Somewhere the little girl she had taken under her care—and the rebellious, carefree teenager she had become under her roof—had vanished.

"I've got a call," she said simply. "Will you come with me?"

Edi looked at her dazedly.

"I have to feed Buczek," she said, nodding toward the creature sitting calmly in her arms. "What should I give him, Auntie?"

"Make him scrambled eggs with cracklings. Kłobuks like that. Then leave him alone," Janina advised. "I'll wait here for you. It's not very urgent, and I could use the help."

The girl nodded and went to her room. First of all, she hid Marek's hoodie—together with the documents wrapped inside it and the phones taken from the attackers—in her bedside drawer, switching them off on the way, just in case. She had no idea yet what to do with them. Then she found an old sweater in a drawer, rolled it into a makeshift nest, and placed it beside the rabbits' pen.

"Make yourself at home, Buczek," she said warmly, setting the kłobuk on the floor. "This is Kicuś and Pusia. They shouldn't bother you."

The creature shook itself and toddled over to the bedding, settling down with visible satisfaction. Edi ran to the kitchen, quickly fried a portion of scrambled eggs in lard with cracklings, transferred it to a porcelain bowl, and carried it back to her room. Then she changed into her work clothes, stroked the leisurely eating kłobuk once more, and went downstairs to her waiting aunt.

"Where are we going?" she asked, settling into the passenger seat.

"To the Grześkowiaks. The ones with the riding stable, not the oscypek producers."

"What happened?"

"I'm supposed to examine a few retirees."

Edi searched her memory. She had heard of that stable before—but where was it? Ah, the Kluczwoda Valley. Janina went there sometimes, usually alone. Occasionally with another vet.

"That's about thirty kilometers away," she said after a moment. "Don't they have some hack closer by?"

"They do—more than one," Doctor Batory started the engine. "But the Grześkowiaks only ever call me."

"Because you're the best?" the girl smiled, though she felt anything but cheerful.

"No. For another reason. But later. What happened?" the veterinarian drove confidently, glancing at her niece out of the corner of her eye. "I know you weren't at Skrab's, because I called his mother after Mrs. Mokrzycka phoned me. Marek didn't come home for the night, and no one can reach him. You weren't answering messages."

The girl briefly recounted everything that had happened. Janina listened without taking her eyes off the road.

"Jadwiga panicked and ran to Emilia," she said at last, "and Fred and Alina are searching the area for you."

Edi frowned and pulled her smartphone from her pocket. The messages were blocked—she must have changed the settings accidentally while marking telemarketers' texts as spam. She dialed her uncle's number and sent a short message: *Everything's fine with me. You can come home.* She sent the same to her mother. A moment later the phone rang, playing the *Addams Family* theme she had set as her ringtone.

"Are you really all right?" Jadwiga's anxious voice sounded in her ear. "Emilia couldn't locate you and she's a wreck because of it."

"Then calm her down. I was in the Heartwood—that's probably why."

"Żywia summoned you?"

"Yes, Mom. We'll talk at home. For now I'm going with Auntie on a call." She hesitated. "If Marek calls—or if he comes to Jodełka… don't trust him."

"I know. Emilia received a warning. That's why she was so upset. Żywia could have let us know you were with her too... but never mind. All right, I'll wait for you at home. Just please, don't get yourselves tangled in some curse along the way."

"We'll try," Edi promised with an involuntary laugh.

"Jadwiga is late coming into her role as an overprotective mom," Janina remarked dryly. "But it's hard to blame her—she has lost years to make up for. And it's hard for a witch to be a mother."

"I don't want children anyway. Nothing but trouble," young Gwerska muttered.

"You'll change your mind someday," the veterinarian assured her.

"Did you?"

"For me it's too late. I missed my moment. Now I would have to renounce being a witch—which is technically very complicated, and besides... I don't want to. I am who I am, and I won't give that up."

"Mom gave it up," her niece whispered softly.

Her aunt looked at her with a smile.

"Yes. Jadwiga fell in love with your father and wanted to be an ordinary woman. To have a husband, children... When you were born, she wrote to me that she had never been so happy,

172

and that if she were to die the next day, she would regret nothing—not a single minute."

A sudden warmth washed over Edi. Her high-school friends usually spoke of motherhood only in horrible terms, declaring, *Kids? Never in my life! I'm not stupid. I'll get a shelter dog, or two cats if I get lonely.* They often shared stories heard from relatives or neighbors about pregnancy and childbirth, always with fear or disgust. Such an attitude was fashionable; they even considered it a mark of modernity. *A woman isn't a two-legged incubator—she can achieve far more than being a broodmare,* they would say with superiority.

"But supposedly she had a difficult delivery?" Edi recalled Tamara's stories, her nanny.

"Very difficult," Janina nodded. "For former witches it's practically the rule. She suffered terribly, and her life was in danger."

"That's awful! She must have been traumatized afterward."

"I don't know," Janina said. "I asked her about it once. Do you know what she said?"

Edi looked at her with curiosity.

"What?"

"She said, 'My God, I forgot everything the moment they placed little Edyta on my belly—tiny and helpless. Such joy flooded me that I felt like screaming, and I felt nothing else. Truly.'"

"Hard to believe."

Janina smiled to herself.

"A simple biological mechanism. It has to exist, or there would be no continuation of the species. It works in all females. After all, what are we humans, if not mammals?"

With that philosophical remark she fell silent, as they were just arriving at their destination.

CHAPTER XI

The Arabian horse stud owned by the Grześkowiak family might not have been anything like the famous Janów, but it did enjoy a solid reputation. It prided itself on impeccably kept, pedigree animals and each year sold several purebred foals abroad, bringing the owners considerable income. The stud's main business, however, lay in renting horses to tourists and film crews, as well as in the regularly organized riding courses.

The estate, named "Konvalon" by its owners, inspired widespread admiration with its charm. Situated slightly off the main tourist route in the Kluczwody Valley, beyond Castle Rock, it featured a birch grove, an apple orchard, and a small yet remarkably clean lake fed by one of the tributaries of the Rudawa River. All the buildings had been carefully integrated into the landscape so as to form something close to an artistic installation.

There were relatively few animals at the stud, but they were cared for meticulously, a fact appreciated by buyers and guests attending events held there. The entire property had been

175

designed and managed with the animals' well-being in mind; a large section of land had even been set aside as a kind of geriatric ward for "retirees." Four aging horses currently lived there, and it was for them that Janina had been called.

Edi had heard of the Grześkowiaks before, but this was her first time seeing them in person. He was tall, flaxen-haired, with a short beard, well-built though perhaps a bit overly muscular. She was slender and long-legged, with captivating doe-like eyes and a storm of russet-golden curls. Had Gwerska not been a young witch, they would likely have struck her as ordinary villagers, no different from others in the area. But as an apprentice witch with already expanded perception, she immediately recognized who she was dealing with—and stepped back instinctively.

"Impossible…" she whispered.

"Why impossible?" her aunt nudged her reproachfully in the side. "You know Żywia, you know the Titans, you know Wo— well, you know who—and suddenly it's 'impossible'?"

Of course Janina was right, but encountering the most important Proto-Slavic gods face to face was always a shocking experience for anyone who could recognize them and was still mortal. Edi had already grown accustomed to Żywia and treated her more like a 'higher witch' than an actual goddess. Here, however, stood Veles and Mokosh in the flesh, looking at her with undisguised amusement.

"I told you she'd recognize you," Janina said with evident satisfaction, addressing the owners of the stud.

"I don't understand," the girl said after a moment, having gathered her thoughts. "You certainly don't need a veterinarian to keep your animals healthy. Come on."

"We don't," Mokosh agreed. "But human bureaucracy does. In today's world even gods must disguise themselves skillfully, so we comply with the rules."

"Neil Gaiman, *American Gods*," Edi murmured to herself. "So it wasn't fiction after all."

"Let's say—not entirely," Veles replied. His voice was deep, hollow, and dark, like the rumble of distant thunder.

"They really all live among humans?" the young Gwerska asked, her eyes darting anxiously from one deity to the other. "Why? What for?"

"Because we want to," the red-haired goddess answered. "It sounds trivial, but we simply love people. We like being among them, even when we can no longer do anything for them."

"What do you mean, you can't?" Edi asked, completely bewildered.

"We can act for humans only when humans believe in us. Faith gives us power. No faith—no miracles. That's how it is," Mokosh said, then turned to the patiently waiting veterinarian. "Isn't she a bit young for a witch? Almost a child."

"It turned out that way. An emergency situation," Janina replied calmly. "My niece has handled what fell on her shoulders remarkably well."

"If you say so... Janeczko, yesterday we had activists from the Centaur Foundation here. They seem to have an appetite for our horses—threatened us with veterinary inspection and the prosecutor's office. We need additional certificates."

"Oh, them," Doctor Batory snorted. "One of those clever types who make good money under the guise of animal welfare. It's tragic what money and the thirst for publicity do to people. Worst of all, both animals and their owners suffer. I know cases that are frightening to even recount."

Veles nodded knowingly. "I know. I've heard a lot about it as well. For now, we're acting calmly—we don't want to raise suspicion, so just fill out the paperwork. If they start playing really dirty, we'll take care of them ourselves. And then they'll regret ever being born. But for now, we lie low."

"Well..." Janina hesitated. "Do you know anything about Asbiel and the Red Spirit?"

"As much as necessary," Veles replied, frowning slightly. "We must stay on the sidelines—as long as we can. If we join such a conflict, the entire country could suffer. It would likely lead to a 'minor Ragnarök.' You know what that means. We don't want that. Besides, we believe you'll manage."

"And if we don't?" Edi blurted out.

The god of magic and prosperity looked at her with mild surprise, as though taken aback that such an insignificant human speck dared speak to him. Then he smiled indulgently.

"More faith, child. More faith. The daughters of Żywia have never given up, even when things seemed hopeless. You are beautiful, strong, and fierce. This isn't the first time Asbiel has tried to subjugate you through a ruthless but gifted human. All right, Janeczko—take care of our retirees. They're what this round is really about. The activists first tried to convince people that we're fattening 'decommissioned' horses for slaughter, and now they want to accuse us of criminal neglect."

"They have no idea who they've crossed," the vet snorted contemptuously. "Fine then. Let's go. I don't have all day."

Edi followed her aunt, carrying the medical bag and discreetly taking in her surroundings. It wasn't just the horses—truly magnificent specimens—that caught her attention. To a young witch's eyes, the entire estate shimmered with magical enhancements and protections. At times she could even glimpse small figures of familiars and household spirits: some cleaning hooves, others combing manes and tails, still others driving away bothersome insects. The workers maintaining the grounds did not see them, of course, and cared little about anything beyond finishing their tasks as quickly as possible. They also failed to notice the dryads sitting in the trees, pointing at them and laughing. From time to time one of the dryads sent a large bumblebee or hornet toward the workers, and then all of them would burst into laughter as the panicked humans swatted at the insects. *Like children,* the girl thought, suppressing a smile.

The thorough examination of the old horses—one mare and three geldings—took quite some time, as did filling out the necessary paperwork. Eventually, however, everything was done.

"That should take care of it," Janina said, handing the completed forms to Veles. "If necessary, give the inspectors my address. I doubt they'll bother you again. And if the activists show up, send them packing."

"It's not easy pretending to be human among humans," Veles said, glancing over the papers. "But between us—it's great fun."

"To each their own," the vet muttered. "It's not my place to lecture you. Enjoy yourselves—and if you need me, I'm at your service."

Mokosh smiled and tied a bracelet intricately woven from horsehair around Edi's wrist.

"Wear it at all times," she said kindly. "In a moment of need, any animal you meet on your path will help you."

"Thank you," the girl murmured, unsure how she ought to address such an important goddess. "It may come in handy—especially now."

Mokosh patted her head like a small child. "Be brave. Many things appear far worse at first glance than they truly are."

One of the horses approached, snorted softly, and nudged Edi in the back with its muzzle. Startled, she turned around. The noble animal gazed at her with large, intelligent eyes, flaring its nostrils and pawing lightly at the ground.

"May I?" Edi reached out and patted the horse's neck. In response, it nudged her cheek and neighed amiably. There was something extraordinary about it—slender, tall, with fine legs and a relatively small head, more like an idealized image from a painter's brush. Its glossy coat was a pale, almost silvery gray; its thick mane and tail were slightly darker.

"You're beautiful…" the girl whispered in awe, running her hand along its neck. "What breed are you?"

"Guess," Mokosh laughed.

Stunned, Edi glanced at her aunt, then back at the horse. She wasn't yet an expert on breeds, but she knew many of them and their defining traits. Judging by its build, the animal was unquestionably hot-blooded and most closely resembled an Akhal-Teke. That seemed improbable, especially since all the other horses were clearly Andalusians—pedigreed, but far more common and far cheaper than the exclusive "golden horses" of Turkmenistan. She walked around the animal, studying it carefully. Finally, her attention was drawn to the hooves—smooth, delicate-looking, unshod, like they had been carved from brown jade. Only one creature could have hooves like that…

"Oh my God," she groaned. "That's—it has to be a kelpie!"

The goddess applauded lightly. "Exactly. His name is Kellus. Take him. He's yours."

"What do you mean, mine?" Edi's astonishment knew no bounds. The horse snorted and nudged her cheek again with its warm nose.

"Yes. Get on—he'll take you home."

She looked questioningly at her aunt, who merely shrugged in resignation. It was clear from her expression that she had had quite enough for one day—first a kłobuk at home, now a kelpie, and on top of that the matter of Marek and his uncle. She had no strength left to protest.

Edi had taken riding lessons before, but this was her first time riding bareback. The beautiful steed was unsaddled and unbridled, wearing only a wide, silky ribbon tied fancifully around its head and muzzle, long and strong enough to hold onto. Her childhood training in rhythmic gymnastics and later jujitsu lessons proved invaluable, as staying on the horse under these conditions was no small challenge. She wasn't even sure whether this kind of riding complied with modern law, but she didn't worry about it. After a while she adapted enough to begin enjoying it.

More out of curiosity than any real need to shorten the route, she didn't guide the horse toward the bridge when their path was crossed by the Wierzchówka stream, swollen after recent rains. She very much wanted to know whether kelpies truly could trot across the surface of water. In principle it wouldn't have been necessary—the stream had many shallows where a horse could cross easily—but the stretch she encountered was fairly deep. For Kellus it posed no obstacle at all. It seemed as though he were running not on water but on a thick sheet of ice, reaching the opposite bank without even wetting his hooves. He also arrived at Jodełka far faster than any ordinary horse could have managed. Janina's jeep appeared in the driveway barely two minutes later.

"Get down," the vet ordered as she climbed out of the vehicle. "We need to talk seriously."

Edi slid obediently from the horse's back.

"We don't have a stable," she noted with concern.

"Not necessary. Nor feed," Janina replied, approaching the magical steed. She parted its mane and pulled something out from behind its left ear that her niece hadn't noticed before—a small bone object.

"What's that, Auntie?"

"A whistle," the vet said, handing it to Edi. "Wear it around your neck and never part with it. Your kelpie will appear whenever you whistle. But never summon him without a truly important reason."

The girl turned and wrapped her arms around the horse's neck. "Thank you," she whispered. "You're wonderful."

Kellus neighed, tossed his head, and trotted away lightly, dissolving into the distance like a wisp of mist. Janina sighed.

"Go inside," she told her niece. "I'll park the car and join you in a moment. Make us some strong coffee."

184

Fred was sitting in the living room, sprawled on the sofa, staring blankly at the screen where another episode of *Game of Thrones* was playing. He looked tired and dejected.

"You scared the hell out of us," he said reproachfully when he saw Edi. "You could have at least called."

"I'm sorry, I lost my head," the girl said, kissing him on the cheek. "I need to make coffee for Auntie. I'll be right back."

She ran to the kitchen. She switched on the electric kettle, put some food into Popo's bowl—he was circling her legs with insistent meows—and took a jar of Jacobs coffee from the cupboard. As she was measuring out the grounds into the coffee pot, Krzywonos fluttered down onto the table, wings beating loudly. He opened his beak and let out a hoarse screech.

"You're hungry too?" she asked him. "Did Fred forget about you? Just a moment…"

She opened the fridge. As always, there was a bowl of raw meat inside, so she took a few pieces and gave them to the eagle owl, being careful not to let him snap her finger with his beak. Then she poured boiling water over the coffee, closed the pot, and carried it into the living room. She still had time to take cups and a plate of biscuits from the sideboard before Janina appeared.

First, the vet downed her first cup in one long gulp, then poured herself another and only then sank into an armchair with a sigh of relief.

"Now we'll talk," she said sternly.

Edi obediently took a seat on the opposite side of the table. She felt like having coffee herself, but for the moment she held back.

"As for Buczek, take it up with Żywia," she said at once. "She told me he chose me and that I was to take him home."

Janina grimaced.

"I suspected you didn't come up with that 'brilliant' idea on your own. I don't blame you for it. Besides, what would that change? Kłobuks aren't too much trouble if they're treated properly. The kelpie is a different matter."

"What about them?" the girl asked anxiously. "What's wrong with kelpies?"

Fred, who had been listening in, snorted with a short, humorless laugh.

"Everything."

"Don't interrupt," his sister scolded him, then turned back to Edi. "They're considered the most malicious demons associated with the water element. In Poland they were rarely seen; under various names they're more typical of the British

Isles and Scandinavia. That doesn't mean they were never here. They theoretically fall under Veles's authority, but usually act on their own. They're dangerous and unpredictable. So be very careful."

Fred straightened up on the sofa.

"Is there something I don't know?" he asked uneasily.

"We were at Końvalon and *THEY* gave her a kelpie," Janina explained impatiently.

"Holy Mother of God! Don't we have enough trouble already?!"

"We have more trouble than hairs on our heads," she admitted. "But gods see things differently than we do. They're like that aristocrat who explains to a serf that he should read more books to improve himself—while the man doesn't even have bread, despite working himself to death from dawn till dusk. It doesn't even register with the nobleman. Not because he's evil or cruel, but because he's never known hunger and has no idea what it's like."

"Let them eat cake, right?" Edi muttered sarcastically.

"Something like that—although those words were wrongly attributed to Marie Antoinette by the propaganda of the time. She never said that," the vet said thoughtfully. "Poor woman, and her poor little son. Emilia knew them personally and tried to help, but… never mind. Let's get back to the present. I'm not saying you shouldn't use your kelpie's help when necessary. Just do it sensibly, and remember that one way or another, you'll never have full control over it."

The girl nodded to show she understood, though her expression clearly showed disbelief. She definitely had her own opinion on the matter.

"Wait, Janeczko," Fred spoke up again, evidently having thought something through. "On the other hand… if *THEY* decided it was a good idea, maybe it really is a good idea. Whatever you say, Mokosh and Veles are gods—and even apart from that, they have immense experience. They've been with humanity since the beginning and know their craft. You can't deny that."

Janina let out a heavy sigh.

"All right, let's move on to other things." She finished her coffee and poured herself another full cup. "You said you took the documents and phones from the people who were supposed to kidnap you. Is that right?"

"Yes, they're in my room," Edi confirmed.

"I'll change and then we're going to the police. We need to file an official report."

"Why?" the girl asked, confused, then fell silent when her aunt looked at her with a kind of pity that was hard to describe.

"So that you'll have something to ask about later. Do you get it now? Come on, use your brain. Think."

CHAPTER XII

"The fundamental mistake made by spell-workers in extreme situations has always been their inability to cooperate with ordinary people on the basis of full equality."

So proclaimed the *Chronicle of the Watch*, a massive tome chained to a pedestal at the very center of that strange place. Only Librarians were able to read it. To everyone else, the thick parchment showed nothing but dirty blotches—nothing more—although there were ways to circumvent this limitation. Edi did not yet know them, but Karol was always happy to read aloud the more interesting passages to her. Who had written the Chronicle? That was unclear; perhaps it had written itself. This particular fragment had lodged firmly in Edi's mind. It was a warning woven into the text—a caution against pride, against underestimating the possibilities that harmonious cooperation can bring. Many matters can indeed be resolved with magic. That does not mean they always should be, especially since the outcome of one spell may necessitate another, and then yet another, ad infinitum. It is easy to make a mistake along the way and expose oneself, which is the worst thing that can happen. For this reason, Janina Batory's decision to turn to the police was entirely sound.

The young Gwerska retrieved the items hidden in the cupboard, topped up the rabbits' water bowl, absent-mindedly stroked the kłobuk dozing in the corner, and ran downstairs.

"Remember to say as little as possible," Janina warned her, taking the things from her hands. "You were frightened, you struggled—wait." She touched Edi's cheek with a fingernail and whispered something. "You'll have a bruise. One of them hit you. You don't know what they wanted from you. Some football hooligans with baseball bats chased them off. There's a Cracovia versus Górnik Zabrze match today; those types could already be roaming the area. No one will check. Plenty of them live in the towns around Kraków."

"Oh yes." Edi knew the local fans well. Although the press called them hooligans and pseudo-fans, often demanding preventive arrests before matches, they were not particularly dangerous. They were more like strutting roosters than real thugs and liked to show that they could be helpful in various matters.

"They took the attackers' phones and documents," the doctor continued. "And told you to go to the police. You have to sell Herman that story properly so he has no doubts. While you're at it, mention that Marek has disappeared—have him send a patrol to his parents. Maybe they'll confirm it, and then he'll be officially listed as missing. If they arrest that so-called uncle of his in the process, all the better; there's already a warrant out for him for previous offenses."

Her niece scratched her head thoughtfully.

"I'll try, but you know, Auntie, I'm a pretty bad actress. I got kicked out of drama club."

"What excuses are those? You're to make the effort, and that's that. Every woman is an actress—only foolish men fail to realize it. That's why they're so easy to manipulate."

Janina glanced at herself in the mirror. She was wearing a blue blouse with a low neckline and lace appliqués, tight black trousers emphasizing her shapely figure. Her hair was carefully styled, curled at the ends, and she had put on tourmaline clip-on earrings and a matching bracelet. Edi knew perfectly well that her aunt had received the jewelry for Christmas from Herman Wiszewski and smiled with a hint of malice. She could not understand what Janina saw in that man. He was so… ordinary.

"Not a word," the doctor warned her, applying cherry lipstick and lightly powdering her nose.

"There was a line in one soap opera: 'Gloria, men are stupid. We can't change that—we can only use it,'" Edi quoted from memory. Alinka, like all nymphs, adored soap operas, especially Latin American ones. Ever since she had moved into Jodełka, she constantly pestered the young witch to watch *Shades of Passion* or *Forbidden Love* with her. Edi gave in whenever she had time, knowing Alinka liked company in front of the television and treating her a bit like a spoiled child one doesn't refuse, just to keep them from crying. As a result, she had gained a passing familiarity with countless serialized Latin American sagas, and the fates of Julletta, Miranda, Afonsina, or Rosalinda held no secrets for her.

"I wouldn't put it that way," Janina muttered, fastening the matching tourmaline necklace around her neck. "I find that whole approach stupid. Let's go. Herman finishes his shift at eight. We have time, but it's better to get this over with as soon as possible."

"Will we grab some lunch on the way? I'm starving—I haven't eaten anything since breakfast."

"Sure, sure. We should manage." Dr. Batory checked her watch. "It's not that late. But no McDonald's or KFC this time. We'll go to the milk bar next to the station—tomato soup and chicken with salad."

Edi grimaced.

"I hate salads."

"Grated carrot will do. You can tolerate that."

193

Healthy eating was something Janina tried to maintain daily for the sake of the household. Occasionally she relaxed her stance, allowing pizza—something she herself enjoyed—or other treats, but she tried to do so rarely. As she liked to say, fast food was harmful even to mages.

Lunch at the milk bar—"milk" in name only, as meat dishes were served there as well—turned out to be quite tasty, contrary to Edi's fears. Immediately afterward they headed to the police station, where they were curtly informed that Senior Constable Wiszewski was just finishing with a suspect arrested by one of the patrols and that they would have to wait. It took over an hour. Young Gwerska fidgeted on her chair, sighing softly, earning reproachful looks from her aunt. Finally, the moment came when the detective stepped out of his office. His tired, worried face brightened at once when he saw the doctor.

"Janinka!" he exclaimed. "How nice to see you! I'm almost off duty—"

Dr. Batory rose from her chair with studied grace, smoothing her hair in a seemingly reflexive gesture.

"Hello, Herman," she replied warmly. "I'm sorry, but this isn't a social visit. We've come to file a report."

The smile on the policeman's face gave way to professional interest.

194

"Come in," he said, indicating the open office door. "What happened?"

"Someone tried to kidnap my niece." Janina nudged Edi forward and waited until Wiszewski closed the door behind them. "The poor thing came home completely shaken."

"Wait," the detective said, sitting down at his computer and opening the appropriate form. "First, personal details. Only one of you should speak. Preferably you, Janinka. It's against procedure, but Edyta is clearly still upset and frightened. She'll give her statement later."

"All right, if you prefer."

Edi obediently waited her turn and then, encouraged by Wiszewski, began haltingly recounting the prepared story. The detective typed, occasionally interjecting with a question. His furrowed brow showed that he was thinking hard. Finally, he looked up from the keyboard.

"You really don't know them?" he asked.

"I'd never seen them before," she assured him. "From a distance, one of them looked a bit like Marek—he had long, fair hair and his hoodie. Oh, and his iPhone."

"Marek?"

"Mokrzycki. A friend of mine. You questioned him about his uncle, Janusz."

"Oh, that case."

"Yes. He's back, you know." Edi asked with convincingly innocent naivety—and hit the mark, because the detective jerked upright in his chair.

"What are you talking about?!"

"Well, yes. He wrote to Marek's dad that he was in town."

"You didn't tell me this!" Janina exclaimed.

"I'm sorry, Auntie—Marek asked me not to…" Edi put on a contrite expression.

Herman Wiszewski rubbed his face with his hands.

"Wait. What exactly did he write?"

"Well…" the girl hesitated. "That he was in town and would get in touch. And then Marek disappeared."

"Disappeared how? When?"

"I don't know exactly when. He didn't show up at the bus stop, he wasn't at Szkrab's place… and when I called his mother, she said he hadn't come home," Janina cut in. "He may be an adult, but Mrs. Zofia was very worried."

The senior constable tapped at the keyboard.

"No missing person report has been filed, and it's too early for that anyway," he muttered, then added aloud, "But given what you've told me, it would be best if I sent a patrol to the

Mokrzyckis'. That Janusz is a dangerous type—I've looked into his record... he actually has a different surname, but it's the same man. If he's shown up again, we need to pick him up as soon as possible."

"Let's just hope he hasn't hurt Marek," Edi groaned.

"Let's hope so," the detective said, trying—unsuccessfully—to sound reassuring. There must have been troubling things in the file he had mentioned. "Let's get back to you. They tried to force you into a car?"

The girl nodded.

"After Julek and his buddies beat me up, you remember, I took up judo, so I'm not that easy," she said. "Still, I couldn't have handled them alone. They weren't born yesterday either." She pointed to her cheek, adorned with an artfully placed bruise, then pulled a bundle from her pocket. "I was screaming for help, and then those fans showed up. They beat them up and chased them off, and left me these. One of them said, 'Give it to the cops.' Oh—sorry..."

"That's all right," the policeman reassured her. He examined the documents and phones carefully. "I'll hand these over to forensics. The papers are probably fake, but it's worth checking. This case seems quite serious. Perhaps you should leave town for a while? Or—" he smiled under his mustache "—at least carry a stun gun with you at all times?"

"But I—" Edi stammered.

"Yes, yes, I know. I know perfectly well that you have one and know how to use it. I didn't pursue the subject last time because I was glad to finally nail those hooligans for something. Now you're of legal age, so you can carry it without breaking the law. And what was, and is no more…" He winked at the girl and turned back to her aunt. "I can arrange protection for her—at least temporarily."

"There's no need, thank you. I'll send her to distant relatives for now. They'll look after her until you catch those bastards or identify whoever hired them," Janina replied firmly.

"If you're sure, all the better—we're terribly understaffed. You may go. I'll drop by once I learn something." The detective picked up the desk phone as it began to beep. He listened for a moment, responding with curt monosyllables, then hung up and looked at the doctor and Edi, who were already standing by the door, with a different, almost alien expression.

"That was the duty officer," he said. "Three young people have just been found dead in a house in Kleparz. Two men and a woman."

***

It was not standard procedure. However, Herman Wiszewski's police instincts had never failed him before, and he trusted them this time as well. Besides, he didn't believe in coincidences or chance occurrences. That was precisely why he had asked Janina and Edi to accompany the team of forensic technicians heading to the site of a potential crime. They didn't refuse. He knew they wouldn't.

He admired Janina Batory not only for her exceptional beauty, but above all for her character and sharp mind. He was no longer a young man and had lived long enough to know what truly mattered in a person. Like any other man, he appreciated beautiful women, but a close relationship only entered the picture for him when he liked something more than just a face and a pair of legs. And in this case, he was more than convinced he had found "the one." The best one.

He also knew she wouldn't faint at the sight of a corpse—though he wasn't so sure about her niece. The entire drive, while seemingly focused on steering his worn-out Opel, he was wondering how to spare that delicate teenager a shock that could haunt her for the rest of her life. More than once he had seen witnesses her age—or even older—react when forced to identify a body. Some, who seemed tough and combative, fainted or burst into hysterics. Others later ended up with psychologists or even psychiatrists. And you could never really tell how someone would react.

"Edyta…" he began when they were already close. "Or would you prefer 'Miss Gwerska'? You're essentially an adult now, since you've received your ID card."

"Oh no. Please talk to me like before, I'm used to it," Edi said shyly.

"Well then… I want to warn you that what you're about to see may be… unpleasant. Even nasty. You've never seen a dead body before, have you?"

For a moment she was tempted to quip that he still didn't know much about her, but she restrained herself.

"No, sir," she answered, then added defiantly, "But I think I can handle it. I'm a veterinary assistant. Do you think it's the ones who tried to kidnap me?"

The detective shrugged.

"I don't know. We'll see. If someone really is hunting you, we have to consider the possibility that he got rid of the hired help once they failed. What on earth did you get yourself mixed up in?"

"I have no idea. I avoid trouble," she assured him. It was obvious he wasn't entirely convinced. Professional experience had taught him that even the closest family often had no idea what their children were capable of or what kinds of ideas they might come up with.

"Mom doesn't know, dad doesn't know, what the kid will think up," he said skeptically. "You're a good girl, but at your age people usually do the stupidest things. You go to Michał Obrędzki's place, don't you?"

"Only professionally. When I assist my aunt. And…" she hesitated for a moment, "a few times I went along as a minder for Tosia Dziekońska, a girl who's friends with his son. They ride a pony together."

"And you haven't happened to run into anyone strange there? Someone unfamiliar, dangerous-looking? That Obrędzki has connections in rather shady circles," Wiszewski glanced at Edi sideways. She almost laughed, but managed to keep a straight face.

"Well, I've heard a thing or two about him. They say he's a 'gangsta,' but to me the guy's cool. He just pretends to be teeeeerrifying. He likes animals and treats them well, and as a father he's a real sigma."

She didn't have to pretend just then. She genuinely liked Obrędzki despite the unfortunate beginning of their acquaintance, and so she didn't share her observations with the detective—though she had several. She was a keen observer, regardless of her magical abilities.

The detective clicked his tongue with mild dissatisfaction.

"You're still very young," he muttered.

They were just reaching Kleparz. Even if they hadn't known the exact address, they would have found it without trouble. The blue flashing lights of police cars were visible from afar. The entrance to the small house was blocked off with yellow-and-black tape, guarded by several uniformed officers. As soon as they got out of the Opel, one of them ran over, visibly agitated. He looked like a high school student—probably new to the force and still unable to hide his emotions.

"Total massacre, sir," he reported. "And these are…?" He pointed at Janina and Edi.

"A witness and a witness's family," the detective said, slamming the car door. "We might be able to identify the bodies right away."

"That would be good. We didn't find any documents, and none of the neighbors know them," the young officer glanced at the nearby houses and added a few curse words without embarrassment, despite the women's presence. "I mean, you know, they say they only knew that someone lived there. The owner rents the place out; the guys are trying to figure out where he is now. In any case, it's not him. One neighbor gave us his name and a description. He's an older man, and the victims are, at most, around thirty—and even that's uncertain."

"At most by eye," Wiszewski muttered. "By eye, a man died in a hospital. We'll see what the pathologist says. You're sure it's murder? Not, say, an extended suicide? Or some kind of accident?"

The young policeman shook his head vehemently.

"Definitely not. You'll see for yourself. Someone just butchered them like chickens. Anyway—see for yourself."

He led the way. The house, a small single-story building surrounded by a neglected garden, was open. Another officer stood by the door this time a woman—rather stocky, with harsh features and hair pulled back into a ponytail.

"Hi, Herman," she said when she saw the detective.

"Hi, Baśka," he replied, shaking her hand. "Who called in the patrol?"

"Don't know. Prepaid phone. They're checking the data. As usual, the operator's cooperation is lousy—stalling."

"We'll need a prosecutor's warrant, otherwise they won't give us anything," the detective muttered. "And the neighbors?"

She shrugged.

"Could've been one of them, but so far no one's admitting anything. And by my nose, no one will voluntarily," she spat to the side. "That's the kind of society we have. And then people complain that the police are ineffective."

"Enough complaining, Baśka," Wiszewski cut her off. "Show us the bodies."

The policewoman looked at Edi with clear doubt.

"Well, if you insist."

For a moment, young Gwerska felt like taking offense—but then she realized something. She'd passed her final exams. She'd recently picked up the relevant document from city hall. She was an adult. And yet she still looked like a fourteen-year-old. If Detective Wiszewski, despite knowing her age, instinctively looked at her like a child, then what about everyone else?

"I'll manage, ma'am," she said, looking at the insignia on the uniform—"Sergeant. I know I look young, but I've passed my exams and I have an ID card. I'm Edyta Gwerska." She held out her hand.

The woman hesitated for a fraction of a second, then shook it.

"Barbara Orzelska," she muttered. "Investigating officer. And don't think you're so mature. People older and more experienced than you have fainted at sights like this."

Edi felt like sticking out her tongue.

"I've been my aunt's assistant for two years," she said instead. "I've helped during surgeries on dogs, sheep, even cows. If I didn't faint at the sight of a prolapsed rumen[23] or a mare's Caesarean section, I'll handle this too."

The policewoman didn't look convinced.

"As you wish," she said coolly, gesturing down the hallway. "Room on the right."

---

[23] Rumen – one of the cow's stomachs.

CHAPTER XIII

The moment they crossed the threshold of the house, all objections became immediately understandable. The room visible through the open inner door was literally splashed with blood. It was everywhere: on the floor, the walls, the broken furniture, even on the ceiling. The air was saturated with a heavy, metallic stench. Not only a professional, but even someone completely unfamiliar with forensic work would have guessed that a fight had taken place here—one that was not only ferocious, but undoubtedly loud.

"And nobody heard anything? In broad daylight?" Janina asked sarcastically, looking around.

Wiszewski shrugged with resignation.

"People here don't trust the police. No one will admit to anything. Hey, you there! Can we come in?" he called out to the technicians at work.

"Basically, yes, sir!" one of them shouted back. "We've already laid down boards, you can come in safely. Kościej hasn't arrived yet, so we haven't touched the bodies."

"Kościej?" Edi looked questioningly at Wiszewski.

"Our new pathologist. Recently transferred from Warsaw—apparently a genius," he explained. "Don't touch anything. Walk on the boards so you don't disturb the evidence."

The bodies lay exactly where the killers had left them. One of the men was slumped against the wall, another lay with his upper body on the couch and his lower half on the floor. The woman was crouched at his feet, as if in the final moment she had sought refuge with him. All three had had their throats slit—each in exactly the same way, with a single precise cut, as if done by one person. And yet there must have been more than one attacker… unless magic was involved.

Edi rubbed the side of her nose lightly with her finger. She had noticed before that this small gesture helped sharpen her sixth sense, as if a witch's sensitivity had something to do with the sense of smell. Yes—she could clearly detect a faint but distinct magical aura. Someone who had recently been in this room must have possessed considerable power, and it certainly hadn't been any of the dead. The sight truly could have terrified someone with less hardened nerves than hers.

Just to be safe, the girl whimpered, shuddered, and pressed herself against her aunt, hiding her face in her chest.

"Are you all right?" the detective asked gently, peering over the doctor's shoulder.

"Y-yes… I'll manage," she assured him in a tearful voice.

"I warned you it might be nasty."

Janina patted her niece's back.

"There, there, don't be a baby," she said sharply. "Take a good look and tell me whether these could be the same people who attacked you at the bus stop."

Edi obediently turned her head, then demonstratively wiped her eyes and took a few steps along the plywood path laid out by the technicians. For a moment she studied the bodies, coming to the grim conclusion that… it really did look different on television. The sight was macabre, and the smell resembled a slaughterhouse—hardly without reason. The flies buzzing all around completed the scene straight out of a horror film.

"That woman and the blond man were definitely at the bus stop," the girl said in a trembling voice. "I'm not sure about the other guy. I didn't see him clearly."

"Good. Now step outside," Wiszewski said, approaching and placing a protective hand on her shoulder. "One of the officers will drive you home; I have to stay here. Janina, I'll drop by once

I know more. I suggest that Edyta not leave the house for the time being."

"All right," Doctor Batory replied curtly. "She'll stay home and study for her exam. True, she won't be taking it until next year, but she can start cramming now. It won't hurt her."

"I'll file a request for protection for your niece. At least temporarily, until we find out what's going on."

Janina hesitated.

"Well, if you think it's a good idea," she said finally. "Something doesn't add up here. I can't think of a reason why anyone would want to kidnap Edi—and with such theatrics. Why? We're not wealthy; everyone knows that, so ransom is unlikely. Blackmail is improbable too—what would be the point? She might have caught someone's fancy badly enough for them to take a risk, but then they wouldn't have hired that trio; they'd have done it themselves, or with one accomplice. After all, she's a petite girl, not Chuck Norris. And no one would murder them just because they botched things for reasons no one could have foreseen. The more I think about it, the less I understand."

"Yes," the detective agreed reluctantly. "But that doesn't mean Edyta isn't in danger. I'll arrange the protection. Even if you're right, I'll sleep easier. Whoever is behind this, as you can see, doesn't… pull punches."

The doctor nodded without enthusiasm.

"As you wish, Herman. For now, I'm taking the girl home. She'll be safe there. We have a fierce dog, and I recently renewed my firearms permit. I have a Glock and a hunting rifle at home. Both legally purchased and stored in a licensed floor safe."

"Holy hell, you never told me that," the detective groaned, visibly shocked.

"And why would I upset you?" she replied calmly. "Besides, Edi didn't know either—until today. You can check the system; I'm not breaking or bending the law. I obtained the permit according to all regulations. And I assure you, I have no Wild West gunslinger tendencies, and my Jodełka is not the O.K. Corral. Something truly serious would have to happen before I ever decided to use a firearm. Trust me, Herman. Have I ever lied to you? Have I ever let you down?"

She softened her voice, subtly tuning its tone to Wiszewski's subconscious. After a brief moment, the detective visibly relaxed, and Edi smiled to herself, discreetly observing his face. The mechanism described by Frank Herbert in *Dune* was very much real, and any witch—even a quite average one—knew how to use it. Let alone Janina Batory.

After returning home, the doctor first took out her set of magical artifacts and a casket of carefully selected herbs.

"Police or no police, we need to secure the house ourselves," she said. "We'll need wormwood, cleavers, sundew, rosemary… belladonna. Good, it's all here. And rock salt, in naturally formed chunks. Damn, I don't have much left—I'll have to go to Wieliczka. But never mind, it'll be enough for now."

"Why Wieliczka?" Edi asked, examining the crystals that resembled quartz. "There are other mines. They don't even mine there anymore, do they?"

"That's true. But that's where the best salt comes from—the best from a magical standpoint. Do you know the legend of Saint Kinga's ring? It's not much of a legend, really. In one of the shafts, truly extraordinary things happen," Janina smiled. "All right. I'll create a protective circle, and you make us a light dinner. Maybe an omelette cake and clove tea."

"Can't I assist you?" Edi groaned in disappointment.

"There's no need. Shoo."

There was no point arguing when Doctor Batory used that tone; any protest simply hit a wall. In the kitchen, the girl found Jadwiga. She was sitting by the window, drinking coffee and smoking a cigarette. A small mound of crushed butts had already accumulated in the ashtray, and the coffee pot was nearly empty.

"You're finally here," she said acidly at the sight of her daughter. "I went to see Emilia about you."

"And?" Edi asked without much interest. She took eggs from the fridge and cracked them one by one into a bowl, added some cream and flour, then reached for the mixer.

"And what, and what… she praised you highly. Said you're diligent and quick to grasp things," Mrs. Gwerska sighed faintly. "But you attract trouble. You focus it. It's a particular talent… if you can call it that. Thanks to people like you, danger can be noticed before it strikes with full force. But it's not safe."

"I should think not."

Jadwiga smoked in silence for a moment.

"I was like that too," she said suddenly, just as Edi was finishing mixing the egg batter. "That's why I ran away after my parents died—your grandparents, that is. I didn't tell anyone anything. I just packed up and disappeared. Maybe I shouldn't have. But I was afraid that if I stayed, I'd bring misfortune upon the rest of the family."

The young girl raised her eyes from the container of clarified butter she was opening.

"So that means I might—"

"Yes and no," her mother interrupted. "It's more complicated than you think. And more complicated than I thought back then. You can't run from it; you just have to live with it. That's why you should never tie yourself to an ordinary

212

human being. No matter what you do to protect him, it will end in tragedy."

She lit another cigarette from the butt of the previous one. Edi was slightly surprised that the kitchen should have been filled with acrid smoke—but somehow it wasn't. A little magic could cope even with the laws of physics. She should have grown used to such anomalies by now, yet they still managed to astonish her. Subconsciously, she still couldn't quite reconcile science and magic within a single framework.

She poured boiling water over the clove tea in the pot and mechanically fried omelettes for a while, stacking the finished ones on a plate and dusting them with powdered sugar. It was Jodełka's house specialty. A veritable omelette cake grew on the plate, later cut into delicious, multi-layered triangles scented with butter and melted sugar. No dietician would have approved such a dish—especially for dinner—but it couldn't harm witches.

Janina entered the kitchen when the "cake" was almost ready. She took a mug of tea, drained it in one go, and immediately poured herself another.

"I've created a warning circle with defensive elements," she announced. "I'm terribly thirsty."

"That kind of magic really dehydrates like hell—and chills you too. Who ever heard of doing it without proper preparation? No one does that off the cuff," Jadwiga grumbled.

Janina shrugged. She uncapped a bottle of sparkling water and drank half of it in one breath. Only then did she sigh with relief.

"I didn't want to waste time," she explained. "If the Red Ghost shows up here, I want to know about it."

She took a knife from the drawer and cut herself a piece of the "cake."

"Very good," she praised with her mouth full. "You're getting better."

Edi put the frying pan in the sink.

"Thank you," she muttered reservedly. "I try. Auntie, am I really supposed to just sit at home and wait for who knows what?"

Janina shook her head with a laugh that sounded like a cough.

"You don't have to at all," she replied. "Ugh, I choked because of my dry throat. I'll give you an amulet that generates false invisibility."

"So what—people will see me a bit and not see me a bit?"

"In a way," Doctor Batory said, lifting the bottle of water to her lips again and drinking greedily for a moment. "People will see you, but they'll take you for a stranger. You'll have to learn not to respond to your name, because someone more resistant to magic might call out to you and then explain that you just resemble someone they know very much."

That sounded interesting. It even carried possibilities that brought a mischievous smile to Edi's face. She finally sat down at the table, opposite the doctor.

"So I'll keep going to lessons with Aunt Emilia as before?" she asked, making sure.

"Oh yes. Of course you'll be fully cautious, but you'll go. Magic is not for cowards or weaklings—you already know that."

"I do, but will Auntie's Herman understand that?"

Janina choked on her water.

"Don't be insolent, you little viper!"

The girl adopted an innocent expression.

"What? He's the 'doctor's boyfriend,' it's already out, everyone knows, so what? That's not cringe. He really adores you like a total nutcase—and he's no nobody."

"Edi! I asked you!" Jadwiga shouted irritably.

"But what's the problem?"

"Drop that 'youth slang'! It doesn't suit you at all, and it drives us crazy! At least it drives me crazy."

"Me too," Janina sighed, resting her cheek on her hand. "Are we really that old? Too old to understand young people?"

"Nonsense," her sister snapped. "It's not old age—it's common sense. Ruining language brings nothing good, including for us. You know perfectly well how important careful pronunciation is when casting spells."

"I know, I know," Janina said, cutting another piece of the "cake," placing it on a separate plate, and handing it to the older Gwerska. "Eat something. You can't live on cigarettes and coffee alone."

Jadwiga grumbled under her breath but obediently took a fork and began to eat. After a moment, Edi followed suit. The memory of the massacre on the outskirts was still vivid, but it didn't spoil her appetite. She had no reason to mourn people who had clearly wanted to harm her, though their deaths didn't make her happy either. She even felt a kind of embarrassment at how little it affected her. Moreover, she couldn't shake the impression that there was a false note in the scene she had witnessed—something like the loud scraping of a fork against a plate during an elegant dinner. It gave her no peace.

"Strange smell…" she said aloud after a moment, wrinkling her nose.

Janina sniffed her slice of "cake" suspiciously.

"Nothing of the sort. It's perfectly fresh. What nonsense has gotten into your head all of a sudden?"

"Not the pancakes, Auntie. That room had a strange smell. Not just blood and the usual things."

"I didn't catch anything unusual," the doctor raised her eyebrows in disbelief. "No offense, but I'm both more experienced and more attuned through centuries of constant contact with magic."

"Of course," Edi agreed. "But you were standing by the door, and I walked up to the bodies along the boards. That's when I noticed it."

"What?"

"That's what I'm trying to identify. At first I didn't pay it any attention, but somehow I remembered that note. It didn't fit with the rest." The girl stopped eating and propped her head on her hands. "It wasn't the first time I'd sensed that aroma. Very delicate and unlike anything else. Or rather—slightly like things, and yet not. A bit like wood ash, a bit like sandalwood incense, a bit like some flower, a bit like earth after rain… but really none of them—and all of them at once. It kept changing while remaining the same. That's the best I can do."

The older Gwerska looked at her sister.

"What do you think?"

"Without a doubt, magic—but not the standard kind. That description rings a bell," Janina stopped eating and rubbed her forehead with the back of her hand, staring into some dead point in space. "A scent not of this world, one moment seeming like one thing, the next like another… if you think, 'It smells like white iris,' you immediately decide it's vanilla—or pine resin…"

"That doesn't sound good," Jadwiga dropped her fork onto the plate. "I once encountered something similar, but in connection with sound. And it ended in a massacre near Malmö."

"Where?" Edi asked.

"In Denmark. Haven't you heard? It was a big case."

"I vaguely remember," Janina finally lowered her hand and frowned. "When was it?"

"At the beginning of the twentieth century. We weren't in touch back then, but I know you were traveling through the Amazon with Fred in those years, searching for the golden orchid."

The doctor grimaced, as if the memory wasn't a pleasant one.

"Damn Amazon. I don't know why people romanticize it so much—disgusting place," she snorted. "If I hadn't truly needed that orchid, I'd have fled within a minute. Never mind. What about the sounds?"

"I heard them back then. I went to Denmark at the invitation of the local Circle as a specialist in runic script. The girls had found old records but couldn't decipher them. From the start I suspected it wasn't just about that. They were nervous, clearly afraid of something they tried to hide from me. I discovered why too late."

"So?" Edi swallowed the rest of her food in one gulp and washed it down with the now lukewarm tea. The story had begun to genuinely intrigue her, and she felt it was connected to what was happening now. "Mom, tell us."

Jadwiga looked at her with a mixture of tenderness, sadness, and worry. Deep down, she regretted her earlier life choices. She had made them to protect her little girl, but they had consequences. She had lost so many years of contact with her own child that it was hard to make up for them. A political career alongside her husband was supposed to compensate for that—but that had failed too. Now her daughter was walking a dangerous path, and she could do nothing about it. Life was unpredictable.

"They were very young," she said. "Their mentors—the ones who formed the true Circle—had all died in a fire at one of their homes. Apparently the blaze was so intense that even metal parts of the building melted, and the firefighters couldn't put it out until nothing but a charred ruin remained. The cause was never determined. The apprentices were left alone. They tried to maintain the continuity of the ceremonies, but they lacked experience and knowledge. They also couldn't establish contact with the local Mother—supposedly it was meant to be Idunn[24] herself. All they had was a boulder covered in runic inscriptions, standing near an old hut at a secret meeting place. The Circle's founder had once lived in that hut and left behind many notes, but none of the girls could read them. I undertook to decipher both the texts and the inscription on the stone—and I was curious myself what would come of it. I worked so intently that I didn't notice night falling. And that was when I heard a melody I couldn't identify, though it felt familiar."

She shuddered slightly at the memory.

"Familiar and alive in its own way, yet impossible to define. I stopped translating and listened, trying to understand what was happening. I think I slipped into a kind of trance. Fideli was the one who snapped me out of it."

"She was there?" Edi couldn't help herself.

Her mother looked at her, momentarily thrown off.

---

[24] Idunn – in Norse mythology the goddess of eternal youth.

"Yes," she said after a moment. "Didn't I say? Fideli was one of the girls who summoned me. Very young—only a little older than you are now. She grew up in Denmark and was recognized there by one of the Danish Sisters as promising material for a future witch. As it turned out—rightly so."

"All right, all right, what happened next?" Janina asked impatiently.

"She broke my trance in a way both old-fashioned and effective—by splashing my face with cold water from a bucket. She was desperate and terrified, shouting that 'something had possessed everyone.' From her cries I gathered that whatever was happening was taking place beneath the Øresund Bridge. I thought perhaps a troll had appeared—there are more of them in Scandinavia than anywhere else, and bridge areas are their favorite territory. But it wasn't a troll."

"Then what was it?"

"I don't know. To this day I'm not certain what happened there. A dozen or so residents were killed—people who, for reasons unknown, turned on one another, though until that day they'd been known for their calm and cheerful dispositions. Several shops burned down as well, but no arsonists were ever found, nor was it established where or how the fires started."

Jadwiga fell silent and for a moment mindlessly crumbled a slice of bread from the basket into tiny crumbs. It was clear that those events still filled her with dread.

"Mom… and the apprentices?" her daughter dared to ask after a while.

"That's even stranger," the older Gwerska sighed. "They were all local girls, yet people swore they'd never seen them before or even heard of them. Their families looked at me like I was insane when I asked about them. Most curious of all—Fideli's family didn't recognize her either and called her a shameless impostor. The poor girl cried so hard I couldn't calm her down; in the end I had to threaten that I'd simply beat her with a stick if she didn't stop bawling."

"That's not very nice," Edi observed dryly.

Jadwiga grimaced dismissively.

"Oh, please. It was just talk. I myself was terrified and disoriented like never before. We had to run, not fall apart like fools. It was truly dangerous there."

"And then?"

"Nothing. I took Fideli to Poland—that was the only idea I had. It was the only country that could have been relatively safe for us at the time. I never discovered what really happened near Malmö."

CHAPTER XIV

Herman Wiszewski did not appear at Jodełka until several days later. During that time, Edi had grown accustomed to the fact that acquaintances she passed treated her as a stranger—and she even found it amusing, especially when they stopped her only to apologize a moment later, saying she reminded them of someone they knew. Interestingly enough, the talisman crafted by Janina Batory confused the senses even of such beings as Alinka, Herta, or Kazo. Only the Titans were immune to it; when they came to visit Jodełka, they recognized their friend instantly.

There was no point expecting that of the detective, so when Edi spotted him through the window approaching the door, she took the talisman off her neck and slipped it into a drawer. After all, the idea was to convince Wiszewski that she was dutifully staying at home with her textbooks, too afraid to stick her nose outside. She waited a moment, listening to the murmur of voices downstairs, and only then went down to the living room.

The detective was sitting at the table with a cup of coffee in his hand, trying to look professional—though only a blind man would have failed to notice that he couldn't take his admiring eyes off Janina. Edi discreetly sniffed the air and smiled maliciously, having caught the scent of a blend of magical herbs known to all witches as "Cupid's Feathers." Doctor Batory might deny it, but she cared about this particular admirer in a very special way. Otherwise she wouldn't be making such an effort.

"Good morning, Inspector," Edi said politely, putting on the demure expression of a little girl.

The policeman tore his gaze away from Janina with some difficulty.

"Hello," he replied. "How are you holding up?"

"Very well, thank you. Though I'm terribly bored at home. When will I be able to go out normally again?" She sat down opposite him and helped herself to a cookie from the platter.

Wiszewski grimaced slightly.

"The case has become even more puzzling than we initially thought," he said. "The technicians ruled out the involvement of third parties. It appears the deceased first fought among themselves, and then each of them slit their own throat."

"That's impossible..." Edi hoped she sounded sincere.

The detective shrugged.

"I admit it sounds like some sick fantasy, but that's what the evidence indicates. Kościej—our coroner—swears no other explanation is possible. They may have been under the influence of psychoactive substances, though we don't know which ones. The bodies were found thirty-six hours after death, and many substances are undetectable after just eight." He set his nearly empty cup down and rubbed his face with his hands. Without asking, Doctor Batory poured him more coffee. "The full analysis will take time, of course, but while reviewing the secured papers I came across some very interesting notes. They suggest there was a mistake. Those people did have a contract— but not on you."

This time, Edi's surprise was genuine. She hadn't expected that.

"Not me? Then who?"

The detective took his wallet from the inner pocket of his jacket and pulled out a color photograph.

"Do you recognize her?"

The photo showed a dark-haired girl, somewhat similar to Edi but clearly older. Both women stared at it for a moment, then shook their heads.

"That's Irena Polik—also known as Renka Candy," Wiszewski said grimly. "Queen of the underworld. Involved in all sorts of dealings, including drugs. She's been seen several times by undercover officers with Marek Mokrzycki. They seemed quite close. And this photo in one of the dead men's notebooks means she was the target, not you."

Edi kept shaking her head, unable to believe it.

"But… I was getting the texts—from Marek's phone!"

"Yes, I know. And that actually proves he wasn't involved," the detective said, taking the young man's iPhone from his pocket. "Look—your number is saved as 'Sweetheart.' Irena's phone is saved as 'Biz.' Probably short for 'business.' That 'Sweetheart' must have confused the hired thugs."

"Then where is Marek?!"

"I don't know," the detective admitted. "I sent a patrol to his parents, but they're gone too. The house is locked, the company has been sold. The new owners know nothing—only the old address. I've circulated their details and photos nationwide, asking for any information. So far, nothing."

Janina tapped her fingers lightly on the table, her brows drawn together in a silent question. It was clear she didn't like any of this—and that it didn't align with her own conclusions.

"What about that fraud pretending to be Marek's uncle?" she asked at last.

Wiszewski spread his hands.

"The man matching his photo and carrying a Swedish passport under the name Olf Rødtspøgelse left Poland for Ireland on a flight from Balice two days ago."

"What?!"

"There were no grounds to detain him. The warrant is for Janusz Mokrzycki, and people do resemble each other sometimes. We don't have a warrant for a Swedish citizen. I don't know if we'll ever be able to connect him to this case. Forgive me, my dear—we're the police, not Harry Potter's crew."

That remark nearly made Edi snort with laughter, despite the gravity of the situation. If only the officer knew whom he was talking to…

"Excuse me," she said, springing to her feet. "I'm going for a walk, if it's allowed now."

She bolted out without waiting for a reply. Bubek, sprawled in the garden, lifted his head at the sight of her and wagged his tail. She paused. The enormous mutt was clearly puzzled that the young lady had been home so long and wasn't taking him on their usual evening walks. She had often seen him come up to the door and stare at it expectantly. She'd felt guilty then—but a person taken for a stranger couldn't appear in the village with a dog known to tolerate only family members. She crouched down and scratched him behind the ears.

"Sorry, buddy," she said. "We'll go for a walk when I get back. I promise."

She hoped he understood. He probably did—he was a very smart dog.

Once beyond the gate, she quickened her pace. She already had a plan—perhaps mad, but logical nonetheless. Reaching open ground, she grabbed the whistle hanging at her neck and blew softly. Barely a dozen seconds passed before she heard the thunder of hooves, and Kellus appeared at her side, tossing his abundant mane and whinnying cheerfully. She patted his neck and offered him a sugar cube from her pocket. He took the treat delicately, with his lips alone. Edi knew horses shouldn't be given such things—they ruined teeth and stomachs—but kelpies weren't ordinary horses.

"I need to find the Titans," she confided in him. "Krios and Hyperion. Will you take me to them?"

Kellus snorted softly, nudged her cheek with his warm muzzle, and bent his front legs—a clear invitation to mount. She accepted, trying not to think about how sore she'd be the next day. Riding bareback had its unpleasant consequences, as she already knew all too well.

The extraordinary steed, as it turned out, knew perfectly where to go and which routes to take so as not to arouse human suspicion. Once past the municipal boundary, he smoothly picked up speed, racing like the wind and barely touching the ground. Edi clung to the narrow ribbons decorating his beautiful head, silently praying she wouldn't fall. At that speed, it could end badly—especially if her mount decided to buck. But she didn't fall, and Kellus had no intention of mischief.

Things became dangerous only for a moment, when he suddenly halted. She barely managed to stay on his back, clutching his mane desperately.

"What is it?" she gasped.

The kelpie did not answer. He stood with ears pinned back, stamping lightly and trembling all over.

They were on a side road leading into the mountains. Once a popular hiking trail, it was now almost abandoned. From earlier times, a few crude benches remained scattered along the path. On one of them sat a tall, black-haired man in a dark suit. His right hand—adorned with a heavy golden signet ring—rested on a carved cane, while his left idly plucked leaves from a wild rose bush growing beside the bench.

A shiver ran through Edi. She recognized him instantly. Unsure what to do, she buried her fingers deeper in Kellus's mane.

"Don't be afraid, my horse," she whispered.

Woland turned his uncanny eyes on her.

"Welcome, Edyta Gwerska," he said.

Kellus trembled even harder at the sound of his voice and began to back away, but Woland shot him a sharp look, and the kelpie froze as if rooted to the ground.

"Naughty horse," he said. "Were you trying to run away?"

"Don't scare him," Edi snapped.

"Scare?" Woland raised a brow. "Who do you take me for? I don't deal in 'scaring.'"

"Then what do you want this time? I won't sell my soul."

The Prince of Darkness smiled ironically, one corner of his mouth lifting.

"You really are an interesting little creature," he said thoughtfully. "Is there anything you're afraid of?"

"I am afraid," she admitted honestly. "Of many things. I just don't let fear rule me. Or govern my choices."

"That's good. You'll need courage yet. The women of your family have always been feisty, and when they fought, they believed they needed no help. But sometimes such self-reliance can come back to bite."

"I'd rather lose on my own terms than owe you a victory," Edi shot back. "That would be far too costly."

Woland shook his head. He wasn't angry—more amused.

"You have a mistaken idea of me. I won't force you into anything, nor even persuade you. And I certainly don't wish you harm. Good luck in your struggle with forces you don't even understand, little human speck. I'll be rooting for you."

Slowly, he dissolved into the air, vanishing from the girl's sight like a wisp of steam. She felt the tense muscles of her mount gradually relax. She wrapped her arms around his neck and kissed him squarely between his silky ears.

"It's all right, that man's gone now," she said, as if soothing a child.

Only now did she herself begin to tremble, as if fear were catching up with her at last.

"I hoped he'd forgotten about me," she murmured. "That he wouldn't appear again… Oh well. Let's keep going."

Kellus snorted, tossed his head, and moved forward— though with noticeably less enthusiasm.

Krios and Hyperion still lived in the same place as before. As Janina had mentioned in passing, during their absence the farm had been looked after by Juraś Gąsior, an old highlander from the Slovak side of the Tatras, and his son. Both men had some kind of unwritten arrangement with the Titans, though no one but them knew its exact terms. Janina Batory learned of it only after hearing from her niece about the brothers' imprisonment by Woland and deciding to check on their animals—whether they were being fed and whether anyone had taken advantage of the owners' absence to steal them.

It might seem strange that the ancient sons of Gaia, who remembered the dawn of humankind, occupied themselves with something as mundane and prosaic as sheep farming— that they had nothing better to do. That, in fact, was the very first question Edi asked when she jumped down from Kellus's back in front of their hut. She couldn't help herself.

"Welcome, Princess Antiope," Krios said, bending to kiss her offered cheek. "And what's wrong with that? Besides, take a closer look at the sheep."

"Yes, I know they're Border Leicesters[25]. Still, though…"

Kellus snorted and began rolling in the grass like an ordinary horse. Krios watched him with a smile.

"I see you've befriended a hippocamp," he said.

Edi frowned.

---

[25] A valuable and rare breed of sheep, not bred in Poland.

"The hippocampus is part of the brain—the hypothalamus."

He stared at her in surprise, then burst out laughing.

"No—though the name does sound similar. I only just made the connection. I meant Poseidon's sea-horses. These days people call them kelpies. They rarely form close bonds with humans—very rarely—and yet you seem to have tamed one."

"To be honest, he tamed himself. He kept hanging around Wotan and Mokosh's stud farm. I guess he just took a liking to me. Anyway—where's Hyperion?"

"Right here," Krios's brother said, leaning out of the hut's window. "What's wrong, little one?"

Edi sat down on the low stone wall separating the yard from a small vegetable patch.

"I have a favor to ask—of both of you," she said hesitantly. "It's about my friend Marek."

"That elf?" Hyperion rested his elbows comfortably on the windowsill. "What about him?"

Stumbling over her words a little, she told the Titans the whole story. They listened attentively, without interrupting. Only when she finished did Krios ask bluntly,

"Do you think he got himself tangled up in something through that Renka? Drug trafficking, perhaps?"

She shrugged. That had been the first thing that came to mind when Wiszewski revealed his findings. But was it true? She couldn't believe it. Marek had always struck her as honest, guided in life by a sense of justice and a simple, traditionally understood morality. He was definitely not the type of teenage delinquent. He didn't graffiti school bathrooms, didn't litter the streets, didn't mouth off to his elders… No—it was unthinkable. Still, Edi had learned long ago that staking one's life on anyone was, at the very least, unwise.

"Not necessarily," she replied reluctantly. "But something about this stinks. And if you factor in that Olaf—the one they call the Red Ghost—then something is happening that I don't understand at all. I'm starting to suspect Marek was hiding a lot from me. Either way, I don't want anything bad to happen to him. You understand. Even if he isn't entirely innocent."

The Titans exchanged a long look. They spoke telepathically, in a way imperceptible to ordinary humans. Edi watched them, idly wondering how people could fail to see that these were no ordinary highlanders tending a few dozen pedigree sheep and keeping to themselves. They differed from ordinary men like fire from water—in everything: posture, movement, skin that seemed almost to glow, those extraordinary eyes gleaming with gold even in the dark, even the very texture of their hair. And yet no one noticed a thing. To the neighbors they were recluses and eccentrics; to tourists, a curiosity of sorts. Women flirted with them, men eagerly challenged them to arm-wrestling matches, and everyone admired the flock grazing in the hollow visible from the hut, guarded by four enormous dogs.

"Oh, they're some kind of English mastiff mix," the Titans would reply carelessly when asked about the breed. In reality, their four-legged helpers were direct descendants of Cerberus himself—and not without reason did they inspire fear among the occasional sheep thieves in Podhale. Several attempts had been made to poison them, but these ceased once it became clear that the beasts completely ignored food offered by strangers. Two would-be thieves even passed into local legend after trying to deal with the dogs using pepper spray. A powerful brand from a reputable military store had absolutely no effect. The dogs merely licked their chops, then drove the attackers beneath the rocks and guarded them until their masters arrived, baring monstrous fangs at the slightest movement. The Titans never troubled the police with the matter. They simply gave the thieves a thorough beating and let them go, ordering them to put as much distance between themselves and the farm as possible.

Edi watched the dogs for a moment as they guarded the squat, peacefully grazing sheep with their white fleeces and enormous, pretzel-curled horns. As far as she knew, this was the only place in Poland where one could see such animals. Most tourists—utter laypeople—surely thought they were ordinary merinos. But even a little knowledge was enough to see the difference at once. And yet even a professional cynologist would have struggled to identify the breeds that made up the four massive sheepdogs patrolling the meadow. Of course, Edi knew of their infernal origin, but it didn't bother her. To her they were just as beautiful and graceful as the ordinary dogs she dealt with every day.

Watching them, she was reminded of her encounter with the Prince of Darkness.

"Is it possible," she asked quietly, interrupting the Titans' silent exchange, "that all this chaos in my life is Wol—well, you know whose doing?"

She caught them off guard. They stared at her for a moment, eyes wide.

"In theory, it could be," Hyperion said carefully at last. "If he had it in for you for some reason. But it doesn't seem likely."

"Why not?"

"Because he observes more than he interferes. Sometimes he nudges events along—but very subtly, barely perceptibly. Do you want us to consider him a factor?"

She hesitated.

"I don't want you to put yourselves at risk. He already caused you trouble once."

Krios smiled sardonically.

"He caught us by surprise that time," he admitted. "Quite effectively. It won't happen again, Princess. We know how to defend ourselves. And we'll defend you too—don't be afraid."

"I have the feeling he can be very malicious, and that he doesn't care about consequences," Edi whispered. "I'm afraid—but not for myself. More for Marek. If that Olf dragged him into his games, that would mean he's now on Asbiel's side—and that demon has long been said to rival Wo—"

Hyperion raised his fair eyebrows.

"Yes. If your friend were indeed serving Asbiel, he would be in serious danger," he agreed. "The key question is whether that is actually the case."

"We'll find out," Krios added. "Chin up, Antiope. Would you like some fresh milk? We always keep a jug from the latest milking in the stream so it stays cold. Or perhaps you'll have a late-afternoon meal with us? Before you arrived, Juraś brought us a few graylings he caught in the creek. They'll be ready in no time. And for dessert—berries with cream."

"I'd love to," the girl agreed. "That sounds delicious."

She generally disliked both milk and fish, but she'd been to the Titans' farm before, and everything there—even the simplest food—tasted exquisite: dumpling soup, bread with lard, potatoes with sour milk. She suspected this wasn't entirely a natural effect, but she didn't dwell on it. What mattered was that in this humble hut, lacking even a refrigerator or an electric stove, every offering became something magical to her taste buds. And the knowledge that her troubles were now being handled by true experts was deeply comforting.

She only hoped that on the way back she wouldn't run into Woland again. She was beginning to fear him in earnest.

CHAPTER XV

Life had to go on, regardless of everything. The world, in fact, had calmed down. All trace of Marek's "uncle" and his family had gone cold, while Edi's friends from high school were beginning to return from their holidays. In the evenings her smartphone would grow almost hot to the touch. At times she had considerable trouble reconciling her social life with the study of magic, which she tried not to neglect, yet she had decided to nurture her school friendships. She did not want to be only a witch. The life of Edyta Gwerska mattered to her as well, and it was to remain that way.

That day she was utterly astonished when she arrived for her lesson and found the Great Librarian in tears. It was so unlike her that Edi was genuinely frightened.

"Auntie, what happened?!" she cried in alarm, rushing toward her. Emilia stopped her with a gesture.

"Nothing, nothing," she whispered, wiping her eyes. She pointed to the coffee table. "I've just received a letter from…

from one of my former charges, Ludka. She writes to tell me that Janusz has died."

"Which Janusz?" Edi knew two men by that name. One was Marek Mokrzycki's uncle (who in fact went by a different name), and the other was her schoolmate from the band *The Rats*. It couldn't be either of them.

"Well, of course… Ah, you probably never even heard of him. Perhaps you read his articles, saw his photographs in the tabloids, but didn't pay attention to the byline. You don't know the poetry volume *Prince of the Gutter*, do you?"

"So he was a poet?"

"A poet, musician, journalist, former soldier, a gifted photographer… one of us who didn't make it. That happens too. Perhaps he never fully believed what he was told about who he was and what Gift he possessed; in any case, his attempts at training ended quickly. In my opinion they should have been continued, to the very end—but he didn't want that. He preferred to look for another way to live his life, and that, unfortunately, has its consequences. I couldn't help him when he got into trouble, since he himself didn't want my help."

"You didn't know he was dying?"

"No. He didn't want anyone to pity him, so he concealed just how serious his condition was. And besides—even if I had known, I would still have been helpless, and that's what's breaking me."

She took a folded sheet of paper from the envelope.

"Ludka sent me his last poem."

She wiped her nose with an old-fashioned linen handkerchief—she had no use for disposable ones—and then began to read aloud.

My name is Fur
And I am the destroyer of flowers
I have come for you
To drag you there
Where bowls meet their end
Do you already feel the scent of fur
Upon your chest?
This is the end
The ultimate cat has arrived [26]

She lifted her eyes, and sudden surprise reflected on her face. Edi looked around and saw a large, fluffy, black-and-white cat walking calmly through the living room. Upon reaching the wall, the creature meowed silently and vanished without a trace.

"An enchantment," Emilia whispered in utter astonishment. "It created an illusion spell. No training, purely on intuition…

---

[26] Text by Janusz Maciejowski, April 17, 2024 (died May 20, 2024).

What a wasted potential. If only I could talk to it, one last time…"

She dabbed her face with a handkerchief. Edi sat beside her and embraced her comfortingly. She could guess what her older cousin was feeling and was overcome with sympathy.

"Isn't there some way to fix this?"

"Like what?" Emilia looked at her, not understanding.

"Necromancy…?"

"Ah, child," the Great Librarian smiled through her tears. "You're still so naïve. That branch of magic is nothing like people think. Unfortunately, there's an unbridgeable chasm between the world of the living and the domain of death. No spell in the world can help here. I know what you've read, but it's nonsense. You see, a human body after death becomes something like a discarded garment. If we attempt to bring it back to life, it will be taken over by the first minor demon or imp drawn by the magic. Used as… I don't know… a suit, a costume, which might give a fleeting illusion. But anyone who knew the deceased will quickly realize that this isn't their loved one, just some impostor."

"Damn…"

Emilia folded the sheet with the poem, placed it in an empty envelope, and handed it to Edi.

"Give me a moment to collect myself," she said. "Go to Karol; he's probably watching a new film in the Watchtower or checking someone's book. It's his duty today. Have him place this envelope in the men's section, in the writing division. I'll come to you soon; for now, work with him."

"What a job, all entertainment," Gwerska mused. "Though, on the other hand, reading like this all day... it can be as grueling as cramming for an exam."

"Certainly not easy, though there are speed-reading techniques each of us must master. Up to a certain point, it's essential. After that, it's easier."

The young girl looked at the Librarian with curiosity.

"What do you mean?"

"I no longer need to read to know a book's content word for word."

"Nonsense, auntie."

"No. It's a matter of higher-order magic, far beyond what you or Karol can manage yet. Go on. We'll talk about it later."

Edi wanted to say more, but she looked at her aunt and obediently left. As she climbed the winding stairs leading to the Watchtower, a strange feeling of frustration and helplessness grew within her. She had already faced situations where someone had died, leaving a person in deep mourning nearby.

She had experienced the loss of her parents herself (after all, she hadn't known for a long time that her mother hadn't perished in that infamous disaster). Only now did she realize that such things would continue to happen and that nothing could be done about it. Really, why? Who or what had stood in the way?

In the multimedia room, she found Karol, as usual struggling with some fragment of an old text, this time a scroll rather than a quarto volume. On the television screen, an episode of *Game of Thrones* played, the sound nearly muted.

"Arrow, young one," the magic adept brightened at the sight of a guest. "Why so glum?"

"No, nothing," she said, handing him the envelope. "You need to put this in the men's section. A new illusion spell."

"Alright," the boy sprang from his spot with visible relief. "Want to come with me?"

"Why not?"

Edi had tried several times to enter the men's section of the Watchtower, but she never succeeded. Only in the company of the Great Librarian was it possible, which annoyed her somewhat. The Watchtower had its own rules and did not observe gender equality.

"How do you find specific records?" she asked, walking beside Karol and looking at the densely packed shelves and display cases. "It's a treasure trove."

"Ah, it's very simple," Karol pointed to one of the round mirrors adorning the walls. "You stand in front of it and say what you're looking for. The mirror then shows you where it is. Wait… written spells should be aisle twenty-five, sector C."

He located the catalog section and placed the envelope in one of the empty compartments.

"It won't get lost here."

They returned together to the multimedia room, where the Librarian once again collapsed onto the carpet. He never studied at a table like a normal person; he always sat on the floor, even when reading casually, without adopting any gymnastic poses. Edi perched beside him.

"I'm starting to lose my sense of purpose," she burst out. "One of my aunt's acquaintances just died. She's in pieces; I've never seen her like this. So wise, so experienced, and yet she can't help in this matter. What's the point of it all?"

He nodded understandingly and set the scroll on the table.

"I had the same doubts not long ago. Everything has its price. It's no fun being long-lived when everyone around you drops like flies. And this longevity…" — he waved his hand.

"What?"

He adjusted himself on the carpet and leaned comfortably against the sofa.

"Think: you study, work on yourself, endure tragedies, yet with each passing day you're closer to the grave. Because we all die, sooner or later. The world is one big damned cemetery. Countless billions have passed, each with their own dreams, loves, and hatreds. Many were good, valuable people, artists, inventors, thinkers. And what? Nothing. We don't even know about them. Only a memory of a few lucky or truly exceptional individuals remains. And the somewhat less exceptional? Gone. End of story. No one wakes up; their memory dies with them."

"Truly, as you put it, it makes you not want to do anything," Edi admitted reluctantly. "Why bother?"

"I have no idea. I know there's some purpose; I just can't see it."

"Neither can I."

She rested her head on the sofa and stared at the screen.

"Maybe just believing in it is enough for it to exist? Wotan said that without faith, there are no miracles," she spoke after a moment. "The Bible said something about it too. Though no miracle will help this show. I hate it. So brutal, yet childish and illogical. And the characters are unpleasant, even the positive ones. Especially Sansa—I can't stand that girl. What do people even like about it?"

"I don't know," admitted the Librarian. "I mean, you can watch it, but its 'cult status' is a mystery to me. Still, I have to watch. I've already caught four fragments of important incantations and one corrupted spell. That's a potential danger."

"Yes, because if someone believes..." Edi agreed. Suddenly, something occurred to her. She straightened, eyes fixed on the screen where Jon Snow was verbally sparring with Daenerys Targaryen. Her thoughts began racing at a pace barely manageable. Faith. Yes. It truly was key. Ordinary people generally cannot control what they believe. Mages have the ability to work on the very mechanism of this phenomenon. She knew it, though it hadn't seemed so important before. Yet it was. What had she felt that day, when an unknown force passed through her hands, helping Tosia Dziekońska take her first independent step in years? Had she not, for a moment, believed she had the power to heal her? And that meant she could do more. Much more.

"Charlie, apologize to auntie for me," she said, springing to her feet. "I need to check something. I'll be back... in the afternoon."

"Alright," Karol watched her with restrained interest. "Whatever you plan, good luck," he added, his tone implying, "I'm discreet and asking nothing."

"Thanks."

Edi made her way to the PKS bus stop almost at a run. She was nearly there when someone called her by name. Lifting her head, she saw a low-hanging cloud, and from it poked out the kindly face of Alosza.

"Hey there, missy, where's God leading you?" the friendly sylph asked.

"Kleparz 119," she replied. "Could you give me a lift? It'd be faster."

"Sure. Hop on," Alosza held out his hand. Grasping it, she climbed onto the cloud, which immediately accelerated its flight. "Whatever you need to do, hurry. In about an hour, there'll be a downpour over Krakow, and a really violent storm."

"I'm not made of sugar," she assured him, crouching beside him. Clouds controlled by demonic operators made for a fast and reliable means of transport, but riding on them meant sitting on something more like a wad of damp cotton than anything else. Sylphs felt perfectly at home in such an environment. Humans—not so much.

"Seriously? To me, you're sweet," Alosza smiled. "If only I were younger… and unmarried."

"By the way, how's your family?"

"Thanks for asking. Katia's getting her license soon and will have her own cloud," he said, frowning slightly. "Unfortunately, Rodion and Oleg don't want to continue the tradition. Both claim they don't want to end up with rheumatism or emphysema in old age. You know, our occupational hazards."

"So what will they do?"

"They're going to college. Oleg wants to be a synoptic, and Rodion to work in television," Alosza shrugged. "For now, that'll probably suffice, and what happens next, who knows."

Edi looked at him with sympathy. She knew how much family tradition meant to someone like him, yet she also understood his sons. The world was changing, and they wanted to keep up. They had the right, even if they were supernatural beings.

"Maybe they'll change their minds," she tried to console Alosza. He didn't seem convinced, but he didn't pursue the subject.

"The Old Town," he said, gesturing toward the buildings. "You're almost there. I'll hide behind the doors so you can safely get down, and I'll add a bit of fog just in case."

Thanks to his skill, Edi could safely jump off the cloud without attracting anyone's attention. She waved to the sylph and walked quickly toward her destination—Finn Bergstrand's apartment.

Fideli opened the door and smiled warmly at the unexpected visitor.

"Hello, min älskling," she said. "It's Swedish for 'darling,'" she added, explaining. "I've spent so much time in Poland that my native language feels strangely foreign now. I recently took on a Swedish book translation for Draggonspire Publishing to earn a little extra. That's what I'm working on right now."

"Oh, I'm so sorry," Edi blushed. "I didn't mean to disturb you."

"Not at all. It's actually good you came—I need a break. This translation is really wearing me down," the Swede stepped back, letting the girl in. "Give me another fifteen minutes, I'll finish the chapter and make us some hot chocolate."

She pointed to the open door to the room, turned into the translator's workspace, with papers scattered over the desk and an open laptop.

"Of course I'll wait," Edi said cheerfully. "I'll sit with Finn. How is he?"

Fideli's bright, freckled face clouded.

"As usual, no change," she replied shortly. "Sit with him and tell him the latest gossip. That's what I always do. Apparently, people in comas hear everything said around them."

"Apparently," the young Gwerska said, heading to the bedroom where she knew Finn lay in catatonia. She had visited him before. At first, with surprise that anything could have felled such a strong and experienced mage. Then with hope that "this time he'll surely improve." Finally, out of habit. Nothing changed. Finn lay motionless, pale as a wax figure, and only a witch's perception could detect a spark of life. She stroked his cold hand.

"We'll try…" she whispered. She pulled her smartphone from her pocket and found a message from Karol: *"One hand on the back of the head, the other on the forehead, and go for it."* She was supposed to help Szkrab, but he could wait. What if she only had one chance, once in a while? It could be. After all, she was still learning; her title and status as a fully-fledged witch were far off. She had little control over her powers. When Emilia taught her simple manipulations through basic spells, it felt like trying to hammer a nail into a wall with a slippery, fifty-kilogram sculpture. Whether she could handle this now, she had no idea. But she had to try, no matter the cost. She already knew the dangers of abusing her powers, yet she was determined to risk it, whatever the consequences.

For caution, she glanced toward the bedroom door and stripped naked. She knew that to intensify her efforts, this was necessary; in this, the legends were right. She knelt by the bed and held Finn's head in her hands. It felt heavy as a stone while she tried to concentrate and connect with the primal forces of nature. Only this could allow her to achieve something beyond turning a leaf into a fly—a feat that had already cost her much. She felt it might be possible to move to a more advanced stage otherwise, but Emilia had been relentless.

"If you don't learn to perform such simple tricks lightly, almost effortlessly, you'll never be a proper witch," Emilia had said sternly. "It's like learning multiplication tables before tackling analytic geometry. Or like laying a foundation before building a house."

She was probably right, considering her experience, but Edi's patience was being severely tested. She felt she was learning nothing useful and merely wasting time. Especially now, she could have used some precise skills, yet she had to rely solely on instinct.

It seemed like hours passed before she felt something happening. Her awareness began to expand, encompassing larger areas of space-time, and her hands heated up. Glancing at them, she saw they glowed with a soft yellow light and knew she was on the right track. Ignoring the growing heat, she closed her eyes and focused all her power into a single point. She felt her tense muscles harden to an almost impossible state, and herself become stone, concentrating the greatest powers of the surrounding world. The heat became unbearable. When mortal panic finally took hold, she no longer had the strength to break the connection.

Something like an electric shock tore her from that peculiar state. She collapsed onto the carpet, soaked with sweat, gasping for air. It felt like a monstrous corset crushed her ribs and spine; for a moment, she could see or hear nothing. Then the world slowly returned, reluctantly.

"What on earth are you doing, girl?" Fideli, surprised, stood in the doorway with two mugs of hot chocolate. Her voice broke into a gasp, and the cups slipped from her hands, shattering on the floor and splattering the fragrant liquid everywhere.

The young adept looked at the bed. Finn was still there, but his skin had regained almost normal color, his eyes were open, and his gaze was attentive. Slowly, he turned his head toward Edi, who was awkwardly trying to cover her nakedness, and toward her partner, utterly astonished and frozen like a pillar of salt. He smiled faintly.

"How are you?" he said.

THE END

www.ingramcontent.com/pod-product-compliance
Lightning Source LLC
Chambersburg PA
CBHW031056020726
47495CB00007B/1911